ASH

SPEED DATING WITH THE

DENIZENS OF THE

UNDERWORLD

BOOK TWO

C.D. GORRI

NAUGHTY NIGHTS PRESS LLC• CANADA

ASH

SPEED DATING WITH THE DENIZENS OF

THE UNDERWORLD

BOOK TWO

COPYRIGHT © 2022

C.D. GORRI

ISBN: 978-1-77357-348-9

978-1-77357-349-6

PUBLISHED BY NAUGHTY NIGHTS PRESS LLC

COVER ART BY KING COVER DESIGNS

ASH

**This Demon is about to get schooled
by a human!**

Sunday school teacher, Gabriella Keen, is
looking for Mr. Right. What happens when
her perfect match is from Hell? Literally.

The Demon of Lust is on the prowl. When
rumors spread that Ashmedai is looking for
a mate, everyone wants a chance to be this
Prince of Hell's main squeeze.
Can this Demon find love with the curvy
goody two shoes?

*Ash is book two in the Speed Dating with
the Denizens of the Underworld shared
world, filled with lustful demons, goody two
shoes shifters, and more.*

DEDICATION

*To everyone who has ever had a first, a
last, an everything. You know there will
never be another in this whole crazy
universe, and you're fine with that, which
makes you not only lucky, but one brave
individual.*

Keep on loving with all your soul.
It's worth it.

Del mare alla stella,
C.D. Gorri

PROLOGUE

GABRIELLA KEEN LOOKED over her lesson plans to make sure they were in line with the approved curriculum she received from Fr. Perez. Her old pastor from Saint Rose of Lima Catholic Church, where Gabby herself took Catechism class all through grammar and high school, was a stickler for rules.

ASH

She knew them well enough and had a wonderful lesson all down and ready for her eager class of first graders. They were preparing for their first Holy Penance, confessing their sins before making their First Holy Communion the following year. It was a very exciting time for young Catholics, and Gabby was more than happy to be a part of it.

Of course, there were things about organized religion she did not exactly agree with or follow, but she'd always found the history of the Catholic Church, and the traditions, simply fascinating. Being part of a community of faith was comforting, and as a CCD teacher, she was giving her students that sense of belonging they would hopefully carry with them throughout their lives.

"Everything needs a foundation, little bit."

Her father's words came back to her as she closed her lesson plan book and replaced it on the small desk she'd had since her own school days. Her bedroom felt the same, despite the fresh paint and new bedspread. Like dreams and wishes, family and support, unconditional love, and a hint of sadness for those she'd lost. Coming home was supposed to feel that way, she supposed.

The warm, dry California breeze drifted in from the open windows and she sighed. Gabby was trying to find contentment with her life, but it was difficult with her being so unsettled. Running back home with her metaphorical tail between her legs was not exactly where she wanted to be at this stage of her life. But some things could not be helped.

Sad sigh.

Gabby had left home right after college hoping to find herself, her place in the world, but so far, she'd had no luck. She was a good person, or at least she tried to be. Being a teacher was the one thing she always thought she'd wanted, but lately, she was not so sure.

Something was different inside of her. It was like something had changed. Her way of thinking perhaps, or her long term goals. Gabby didn't know for certain. Even worse, she was almost positive she was sick.

A suspicion she'd been too cowardly

to confirm or deny with a trip to a doctor or hospital. She'd been having headaches and stomach pains. Both were highly unusual for Gabby, who never even caught a cold. It was like she felt itchy all over, but it wasn't her detergent or lotion. That indeterminable *itch* was coming from the inside.

This was not how her life was supposed to go. She was supposed to be a teacher, find a husband, get married, and have a bunch of kids. So far, none of that had panned out. Finding a permanent position with her degree in elementary education had not been as easy as Gabriella had expected.

She'd spent the last few years hopping around from state to state, trying to fit in, to build a life.

But how could she do that filling temporary positions?

All she'd ever wanted was to make a home for herself. Her father had moved them from their New Jersey home to California after her mother had died when Gabby was still a baby. It was strange, but not bad. Never that. Especially when he met Mim.

The wonderful woman her dad had met in LA was a terrific stepmother to Gabby. After she'd married Gabby's dad, she made a home for them here in the suburbs of Los Angeles. Her father had been as happy as Gabby had ever seen in those days.

She loved her stepmom too. The woman had adopted Gabby, and she remained in California with her after her father had passed away. She'd been just eight years old when her stepmother, Mariah Bailey Keen, had told her the terrible news. But Gabby's childhood was wonderful despite the tragedies. Her new mom raised her like she was her own flesh and blood, and she never wanted for anything.

Still, Gabriella had grown into a restless young adult, and she had moved to the opposite end of the country right after college. Hoping to find herself in the place she'd been born. New Jersey held no answers, and finding a permanent position proved difficult.

Her latest job was just before Christmas at a posh preschool in Manhattan. The position had ended just after the new year with the return of the teacher who'd been out due to maternity leave. She was cold and lonely all by herself on the East Coast, and Gabby had been positively delighted when her stepmother invited her to come back home for a while.

"I miss you, Gabby girl, come home."

Mariah's plaintive message had greeted her after a sad New Year's Eve spent alone in the tiny rental she could barely afford. That voicemail had given her the courage to buy a one way ticket back to Los Angeles. Gabby hadn't found what she was looking for where she'd been born. Maybe she'd been wrong about where to look, after all.

Hermosa Beach was about thirty-five minutes outside of LA, depending on the traffic. It was a really nice place to grow up. Their home was a sprawling ranch her stepmother had already had when they first moved out there. It was worth a few million, at the least in today's market. Mariah, or Mim, as Gabby had called her after her father married the lovely woman, owned her own real estate company. She'd worked very hard for the fortune she had.

Considering Gabriella had no money and no one else she called family, she accepted Mim's invitation to come home immediately. It was a much welcomed respite to be invited back to the warmth and sunshine of the last place she'd lived with her dad.

Money was always going to be a problem for her, but she never questioned Mim's love for her. Still,

ASH

Gabby refused to take money from her. Her stepmom had tried time and again to give her funds, but Gabby was stubborn.

She just didn't want anyone to bankroll her life. She couldn't do that, preferring to earn her living herself. It was one of the things Dad had instilled in her.

"Work hard for what you have, and no one can take it away."

The world was a rat race, and Gabriella simply did not have the constitution for it. Especially not now.

Oh no.

What if she really turned out to be sick?

Gabby was always a *goody goody*. She didn't drink, didn't smoke, paid her taxes, went to Church.

Why was this happening to her?

The moment of self-pity made her feel terrible, and Gabby quickly asked God for forgiveness. There were so many suffering in the world right now. People with families and incurable illnesses. She should not whine or complain. Not when she had it so good, relatively speaking.

Her old room at Mim's was remarkable. Twice the size of the apartment she'd been living in. Hermosa Beach was a great place to live. Always sunny and warm, even if she felt chilled most of the time.

She knew people who weighed success by how much money you made or how thin you were, or who you were dating. Heck, the tuition at the preschool where she'd last worked had cost more per annum than her yearly college tuition. Certainly more than they paid their staff.

It was insanity. But Gabby didn't care about money. Or the size of her waist. Not really.

She just wanted to be healthy and to enjoy her life. Even if she was destined to be alone. Gabby had her work. She loved teaching children. The little cuties went straight to Gabby's soft heart. She simply adored kids. Once upon a time, she couldn't wait to have her own brood.

Sigh.

Her hand went over her abdomen as the tension she'd felt all day squeezed hard in that moment. Darn it. She'd always thought she had more time.

Doubts assailed her, and she frowned, tapping the notebook with her short fingernails.

There was no reason to be morbid, was there?

After all, she did not know if she really was sick.

Gabby wanted to cry at the wastefulness of it all. She really wanted kids one day. With no prospects for potential fathers, and no assurances she was healthy enough to have them, the future was not looking all that bright for her.

Wasn't that a depressing thought?

Long sigh.

"Hello..." Gabby clicked the little green symbol, and spoke into her smartphone.

"Gabby? It's Mim," the familiar voice crooned.

"Hey, where are you?"

"I'm stuck in town and was wondering if you could meet me for dinner?"

"Mim, it's already seven, and I have to teach a class tomorrow."

"Oh, come on! It will be fun," her stepmother replied.

Gabby looked at the time display on the microwave. She had been planning to heat a frozen burrito, but dinner with Mim sounded way better than that. Still, driving at this time of night, even if it was only Wednesday, would take over an hour to get anywhere near LA.

Errrrr.

"Okay, fine," she said, after weighing the pros and cons of it. "Text me the address, okay?"

"Doing it now! And be sure to look nice, Gabs."

"I will, Mim," she returned, rolling her eyes.

As a realtor, Mim had a reputation to uphold, and the perfectly poised five foot ten inch blonde never had a hair out of place. Of course, Gabby, with her much shorter, curvier stature, had to work a bit harder at it, she always managed to clean up nicely. Years of learning how to shop for clothes that flattered her fuller figure and complimented her attributes at hand.

The trials of my youth! Lol.

Truth was, she preferred loose,

comfortable clothing, but she'd dress up for her stepmother. She owed Mim that much. Hurrying to her closet, Gabby pulled out a simple black dress. The kind inspired by Hollywood starlets from the golden age. She grabbed a pair of sling-back heels to go with it, and her full coverage granny panties in an effort to hold in her bulge.

Gabby dressed quickly. She brushed her wavy hair until it looked soft and flowy, adding a little gloss to the ends. The tresses curled around her shoulders, and she noted her natural highlights were a shiny pale gold against the darker chestnut locks.

She used a little mascara and lipstick, and some light powder on her nose and forehead. Gabby had always hated the feel of cosmetics, despite Mim's attempts to get her to wear them. This was a happy compromise.

Ready to go, she hopped into her small hybrid car and headed for the address of the restaurant Mim had sent her. It was one she'd never heard of before, but that was not surprising for LA. These things came and went faster than the wind.

"DeLux Cafe? Must be new," she mused, and plugged in her smartphone so she could listen to her latest audiobook, a really fun vampire romcom by Carrie Pulkinen, and get directions at the same time.

Despite her job as a Sunday school teacher, Gabby was a bit of a paranormal romance addict. She loved anything having to do with the supernatural or occult, especially when they were entwined in a juicy love story.

Where else was a girl like her going to fulfill her romantic fantasies?

Chubby, nerdy, and an utter failure at relationships, Gabriella Keen had resigned to live her life alone. But that didn't mean she couldn't dream. With the new PNR romcom playing in the background, she began her trek to the restaurant.

Who knew?

Maybe someday Gabby's fantasies would come true and some big, sexy man would look at her like she was the stuff his dreams were made of.

Yeah.

Right.

Shhh! She told her inner voice firmly and stepped on the gas. There was no time like the present to start a positive outlook on her life. Her prospects might be nil, but that could change. She just had to believe.

CHAPTER ONE

ASH STARED AT the darkness before him. The soft growl built in his throat until it reverberated throughout his entire body. Shit. He needed more control of his emotions if he was going to get through this.

Everything was different now. Not just him. Even the Underworld was changing, and right before his very eyes. Fire and brimstone gave way to clean streets and sweet smelling air. From a pit of despair meant to reign terror and punishment, to an urbane looking environment thriving with life and possibility. He could scarcely believe his eyes.

But what could he expect when the Lord of the Underworld himself was no longer a miserable old sod?

Happily mated and more powerful than ever, Lucifer had truly done a number on things in Purgatory. Shops, cafes, boutiques, nightclubs, and even an office offering psychiatric counseling to those who needed it were springing up left and right.

Odd.

Very odd.

But not unwelcome.

Truth was, it didn't matter to Ash in the least what the Underworld looked like.

Why should it?

He had a job to do, and he did it well. Protecting its borders and keeping the citizens of Purgatory safe was his purview.

The rest was none of his business. Even if all these changes were due to a certain Lord aiming to please his lady.

Blech.

Why should he, the Demon of lust, a Prince of Hell in his own right, care if Lucifer had found his fated mate?

Let the happy couple do whatever satisfied them. It meant no difference to him.

Nor did he care if Eve and Aphrodite ran a speed dating service for the denizens of Purgatory. It was none of his business.

Period.

The end.

Sounded bloody ludicrous in his opinion, but no one asked him. As such, he wisely kept his opinion to himself. Ash had enough on his plate without angering those two powerful ladies. Besides, there was a rumor of an uprising starting somewhere in the south borderlands.

As General of the Daemonium Guard, Ash was obligated to report the bad news to the Lord of the Underworld. Just another ducky perk. He exhaled, frowning hard.

Lucifer was not known for his tendency to forgive less than perfect results. Now more than ever, he demanded the Underworld be safe from all threats. Ash understood this, and even though he'd only just returned to his position, he assumed all responsibility for the Guard.

The Lord of Purgatory had a reputation for having little patience for error. An impending threat to his kingdom was not to be tolerated. He would demand answers and results, as was his right.

Unfortunately, Ash had neither.

"My lord," he began. "The soulless are stirring. I've had legates reporting unrest in the southern borders of Purgatory.

These officers are trustworthy, my lord. They are the best of their legions, hand chosen by me. Be assured, I am doubling our efforts to squash these rumors and tend to any perceived threat, real or otherwise—"

"Yes, yes." Lucifer waved his hand. "I've read your reports, Asmodeus, but that is not why I have summoned you here."

"Then why have you, my liege?" Ash asked, careful to show his respect for the most powerful being in the Underworld, even if it galled him that Lucifer kept calling him by his more formal monikers. Yes, he was called Ashmedai or Asmodeus, but he preferred Ash. Always had.

His entire perspective had changed.

Not that he could blame himself. After the Demon who had held him under thrall, that evil bastard Molloch, who had been defeated and locked away by Satan himself, Ash had been freed and thankfully forgotten by the powers that be. Indeed, with the end of the Curse of St. Natalis, that which had damned Werewolves for a millennium, by a certain teen aged Werewolf, Ash had been left alone and without direction.

Free for the first time in an age. But with no true purpose. No reason to be. He simply *was*.

And wasn't that depressing?

A shell of his former self, he saw no other options.

Returning home was the only thing Ash could think of that made any sense at all. And so he had. Ash had sped away back to the Underworld. Alone in his manse for weeks to return to his former physical strength. Molloch had left him an empty shell, but soon, he was himself again, if only on the outside.

But even with his strength returned, the home he once knew wasn't what he'd remembered. No more public flaying. No fire and brimstone. True, there was still a hint of sulfur in the air, but it was so faint that even with his Demonically enhanced senses, he had hardly detected it.

The Underworld was starting to look mundane as Hell. No pun intended.

"Asmodeus?" Lucifer called his name. The Lord of Purgatory seemed both amused, and as if he were hiding something. On guard, Ash bowed respectfully before answering.

"Yes, my lord?"

"Enough with the 'my lord' thing, for fuck's sake, how long have we known each other? I think you can call me Lucifer when you are in my office, Ash," the King of the Underworld said with a rather frightening smile.

Ash nodded, though he had no intention of being so informal. He stood, back straight, head high, ready and at attention. Friendly or not, Lucifer was the ruling sovereign. He deserved the utmost respect from all his citizens.

"I said at ease, *General*," Lucifer barked.

He rolled his eyes, probably annoyed at Ash's disobedience, and caused a flash of white lightning cutting across the red-gray skies. It would have been beautiful if Ash had allowed himself the time to observe the phenomena. At the moment, he was trying not to piss off his boss any further.

"Look, you need to snap out of this, Asmodeus. I mean, why so formal? You should be enjoying yourself."

"I should?"

"Yes! You aren't getting any younger—"

"Demons don't really age, as you know, my lor—, uh, *Lucifer*."

Fuck no.

That did not feel right.

He clamped his lips together and tried not to wince at the Lord of the Underworld's raucous laughter.

"There! Isn't that better? Now tell me, Ash, doesn't anything in Purgatory hold any interest for you at all? Aside from hunting down the soulless and tearing them limb from limb, that is."

"Uh, no. Not really. I mean, of course I am grateful to you, sir. I appreciate you allowing me to resume my role as General of the Daemonium Guard," Ash said, stumbling over the traditional courtesies due to his master.

"The current crop of legates is outstanding. I have charged them with keeping their legions and cohorts on point, ready for inspection at any time. They are working in tandem, patrolling our borders, using freshly trained packs of hellhounds to monitor threats. Their prime operative is to keep the soulless rogues at bay and to investigate the rumors in the Southlands."

"You are the best General the Daemonium Guard has ever had, Ash. I trust you to do the job and to do it well. Now, does it look like they will try to invade?"

"It appears that way, sir."

"Excellent! It's been too long since I've seen battle." Lucifer smiled. The Lord of the Underworld clapped his hands together once, then offered a slight fist bump to the air.

He always got excited at the thought of a good fight. Some things never changed, Ash mused, and was comforted by the thought. He could handle a skirmish any day of the week. As long as Lucifer did not want to talk about his feelings, he would be fine.

"Wonderful. Truly. I am exceedingly pleased by your progress, Asmodeus."

"Thank you, my lord. And, please, call me Ash," he offered, bowing once more to show his unending reverence for Lucifer.

From the time he came into existence, he had served Lucifer as best as he could until he was taken and held by the criminally insane Molloch. He'd thought about leaving altogether and finding some solace among the humans, but Ash rejected the idea.

How could he possibly go there after the damage he'd almost caused?

It was a mess, and he was in crisis, truth be told.

A Demon in crisis.

ASH

It was preposterous.

Whoever heard of such a thing?

Angels and Demons all had their place in the multiverse, and none of it was as black and white as it was viewed on Earth.

Fuck it, he thought with an angry growl. Lucifer raised his eyebrows, and Ash shook his head apologetically and waited for him to speak.

"What I meant, Ashmedai," Lucifer said, using another of Ash's longer names.

Sigh.

There was simply no telling Lucifer anything. He did what he wanted to, when he wanted to do it. As was his right.

"I've made some recent observations

of your foul and melancholy mood, and I think you need something *more* to do than simply work. I think you should start dating again!" Lucifer announced with a chilling smile on his face.

Fucking hell.

The Lord of Purgatory had a mate, and now, he was on a mission to ensure everyone else had one too. As if Ash could follow suit!

Didn't Lucifer know Ash would gladly welcome a mate if he had one?

If only.

CHAPTER TWO

THIS DAY COULD not get any worse.

Ash rolled his shoulders, wishing he could flex his wings instead. As a matter of courtesy and a sign of respect, he'd tucked them away for his meeting with Lucifer.

Someone of Ash's stature did not walk around in full Demon mode unless he was looking for a fight. And that was something he had not done actively since puberty.

Oh! Those were the days. When seducing maidens was a privilege, and fighting to the death, never his, of course, was exciting!

Of course, being driven to the brink of insanity by an evil such as Molloch had caused Ash to lose his taste for bloodshed. Besides, he stood little chance against Lucifer. The man was a fallen Angel. He had a set of massive wings himself, not to mention stores of more magic and power than Ash or anyone else in Purgatory possessed.

Ash sometimes wondered if Lucifer missed Heaven at all. He was a Demon and knew little of such things. They dwelled in the same place, but they had little semblance between them. Unlike Angels' feathery wings, Ash's own were sans feathers. He also grew horns and a tail, as was the case with a great deal of the Demon born denizens of Hell.

Full Demonic regalia was only appropriate in wartimes. However, Ash found his Demon surging forward at times of great emotional turmoil, intense passion, irritation, and when prepping for a fight or battle. Definitely not cool to go all Demon in Lucifer's office.

Not to mention it would be a huge *fuck you* to the most powerful being Ash had ever met.

Wasn't it Lucifer who had ultimately saved him?

He owed him his life, and a little

respect went a long way in his world.

Not to mention the fact, it was hard to travel amongst normals when in Demon mode. Ash was not someone who could easily blend with the crowd with his bat-like wings and his short, but deadly, curved horns that protruded from either side of his head. Those were exceedingly sharp and capable of poisoning a foe if scraped or impaled during battle.

Okay, fine.

He admitted he was rather proud of them. They were quite even in size and shape and could prove fatal to his enemies. Perfect, in his opinion.

He also had quite the tail. Protruding from his lower back was a long, powerful appendage that was extremely flexible and strong, with a razor sharp point that exuded the same poison as his horns, if triggered. Another reason he was a cut above the average Demon.

It was rare for a creature, a Demon especially, to be in control of his appearance. Not to mention when or where his or her venom was released. But Ash had that power, and more. If he willed it, his venom could eat through skin, muscle, and bone when it came into contact with an aggressor's bloodstream. The agony his venom could inflict was quite terrible, or so he was told.

Immunity was a fringe benefit of having it, he supposed. Still, it was not his favorite attribute. Flight had that distinction. With his ability to wield magic, the talent to summon and control fire running a close second.

Ash had an enormous eighteen-foot wingspan and could soar at top speeds carrying heavy burdens. And yet, all his strength, agility, and magical gifts were somehow not enough. Not anymore. Molloch had done something unthinkable. He'd caused a Prince of Hell to question his existence.

What fucking conundrum!

"Asmodeus, did you hear what I said?" Lucifer asked, and Ash could tell he was annoyed.

"Dating? Absurd," he replied without thought. "Um, I mean, I am not looking for a bedmate, my lord."

"I did not suggest you visit a brothel, Ash. I am talking about a deeper, more meaningful relationship with just one person. Your mate, Asmodeus. I think you should consider this. It is possible, you know."

Did he know that for sure, though?

Ash nodded respectfully at Lucifer, but the idea now spoken had him quite perplexed. True, he was lonely. But dating sounded absolutely horrifying. Much as he hated to refuse Lucifer anything, it was not something he was willing to do.

"Thank you, my lord, but I have no desire to sip cocktails at the café and pretend an interest in the parade of supernaturals searching for someone to share a bed with. No disrespect intended."

"None taken," Lucifer replied,

smirking. "And what of our fine local citizens? No one special there?"

"Ah," Ash said, clearing his throat. "Let's just say I am steering clear of both Goddesses and Demonesses in residence. I have burned more than one bridge in that respect, and do not want to perpetuate any myths about my reputation."

"But that rep was well earned. Gave you the moniker Demon of Lust, did it not?" Lucifer baited him, but Ash refused to rise to it. "Besides, I thought those rumors about your disposal of Sarah's seven husbands quieted down long ago."

"Hardly," Ash barked, unable to resist the opportunity to put that nonsense to bed. "Sarah was some piece of work, let me tell you. For the record, I never killed any of those lucky bastards. They simply deserted her and blamed me. More like the Demon of gullibility!"

He'd been young then, but it still stung that Ash had been taken for a ride. And by a woman who'd managed to both marry and lose seven men. In the end, he was unsure who was worse, her exes or her!

"Ha! And all feared your jealous wrath for eons after! You poor fellow, being lusted after by throngs of women and dreaded by rivals for their affection. Must have been awful," Lucifer said with false sympathy. The Lord of the underworld laughed aloud. Something that was also new and unusual, but not unwelcome. Even if it was at Ash's expense.

"Yes, well, now that's over with—"

"Seriously, though," Lucifer turned suddenly serious. "I know about what went down with Molloch and that little Werewolf from New Jersey. It was bad, Ash, but you pulled through. You didn't let that evil bastard corrupt you. But I am sorry for you. It cost you some of your heart."

"Molloch is a vile blight on the universe, Lucifer. There is no denying that. But the truth is, I didn't love Grazi. I admired her, respected her, but it was not love," Ash reflected with an uneasy sigh, the ache in his chest still there despite his having realized what he'd felt for her was respect and a deep regard.

"Still, torturing her fated mate—"

Lucifer grimaced and shook his head.

Ash nodded, allowing the familiar shame to flow over him and ebb just as quickly. He'd come to terms with it, but he was done explaining.

The past was complicated. His role in the recent Wolf activities was not all together favorable, but in the end, he'd managed to undo the damage and help their cause.

Did it justify the means?

That sort of thing was above his paygrade. Judgment was reserved for other ethereal beings. Not for Ash.

"It was the only way to save her," Ash replied succinctly. Even if he had a hard time convincing himself that was the only reason he'd done what he had.

"Grazi's mate understood why you did

it, Ash. Good man, that Ronan Madden. Good Wolf too. I am sure the girl forgave you as well."

"Indeed," he replied.

It had hurt Ash. The entire thing with Grazi, Ronan, and the others. But it was not love.

Never love.

How could he ever be worthy to feel that of all the torturously human emotions?

No matter how much he wanted to.

Demons were not meant to feel the glory of love in all its purity. He was no Fallen Angel like Lucifer, and he was not a Shifter either. Loneliness was his only destiny. Ash, Asmodeus or Ashmedai as he was sometimes called, was a Demon. And he meant that in the foulest, most despicable use of the word.

He was born of Hell, cast into Purgatory, and had to fight and claw to claim his station there. A true Demon with the ability to pass among humans was coveted and rare. It was what elevated him among the others and helped make him a Prince among his kind.

"I know your time with Molloch has changed you, Ash," Lucifer said, interrupting his train of thought. "You are not all transformed, Asmodeus. Some of you is still in there, I'd wager. That part that loved life so and lived with such vigor. I am certain with the right provocation, in this case I mean a female, you will find your appetites renewed. Speed dating, old man, that is your opportunity!"

"I'm afraid I have lost more of myself, Lucifer, than even you can see. I am destined to be alone now, as I ever was," Ash whispered.

"No, my friend. That carefree spirit that made you such a successful Prince of Hell is still there. You are not to be alone forever. Not now that I've found my own happiness. I forbid it!"

"If anyone could banish loneliness, it would be you, my lord," Ash said and grinned. "But I deserve it. I do. I've done terrible things. I don't know how to come back from that. Not sure I want to."

"Should I have you guarded? Watched? Do you need a doctor? Chloe says I need to be more mindful of others—"

"No, my lord, I'm not suicidal. I fully intend to go on living here, in Purgatory, changed as it is."

"My mate prefers things this way," Lucifer said, looking out of the window from his office. "I admit, it is a might nicer. Don't you think?"

"Perhaps," Ash said, shrugging. He did not care one way or other.

The fire and brimstone bit was a tad overdone. The skyline was clearer now, changing from reds and yellows to blues and grays depending on time of day and season. Of course, there was always the odd flash of lightning, but that had more to do with the temperamental god, Zeus, than the actual weather.

Beneath the striking firmament of the Underworld, teaming with Angels,

ASH

Demons, Gargoyles, and other various winged creatures and Shifters, there were modern, urbane developments. Houses, cafes, and shops lined the streets, most of the homes were quaint and village like. Lucifer's castle still stood as befitting his stature.

Ash's old residence had been demolished in his absence, but he owned a fine manor now. Appropriate for a Demon of his rank. It stood apart from the others, outside the center of things, which had always seemed too crowded for him. He enjoyed his privacy, if not his solitude.

Purgatory had truly become something incredible. A thriving community, not just a weigh station of sorts. The change the Underworld had gone through was really quite dramatic and all for the love of a mate. Unbelievable. Though, truth be told, Ash was envious of Lucifer. Of the joy he'd found with the coming of his soul mate.

"You know, change is not always bad, Ash."

"That is true for some. But I have no place in this new world of yours, Lucifer. I came here today to ask you to send me away. Send me on a mission, somewhere far away, in the pits perhaps? I can't do *nothing*. We both know I do not deserve to be here, in my castle, mingling with the lot of you. I am far too tainted now, Lucifer."

Silence encompassed him as the Lord of the Underworld considered his request. It was bold to ask anything of

Lucifer. He knew that, but Ash could not bear the loneliness anymore. Not when new couples were springing up everywhere he looked in Purgatory these days.

There was a time when Ash had believed in the Fates and looked forward to their matchmaking for himself, but his time in captivity and bound to the Demon Molloch had changed him.

That evil creature had made Ashmedai the messenger of his evil plots. Poisoning his brain and using Dark Magic to control another Demon was foul work, indeed. In the end, Ash had defied him at great cost to himself, but it had been worth it.

The teen Wolf he'd grown to care for had defeated the curse. Lucifer then caught the beast while Molloch was distracted by the Werewolf rebellion, and thereby freed Ash. The thin scar visible from his left armpit to his hip was all that remained of his plight. A tiny reminder of his cruel past.

And so, here he was now. Back home in the Underworld.

Among friends.

And yet, so very alone.

Ashmedai did not deserve happiness. He owed penance for his crimes, though committed against his will. Ash knew that and would live out his long existence trying to make up for it. He had no other recourse.

"Is this your true wish, Ashmedai?" Lucifer asked.

Unable to respond for the lump in his

throat, Ash nodded once. A short, quick movement as he sealed his own fate.

"Then," Lucifer stated slowly. "I have a task for you, Ash. A job, if you will. And I will brook no refusal." Mellowed somewhat with his mating, Lucifer was still Lucifer. Powerful and used to getting his way, mated or not. Ash might be at a crossroads in his own existence, but he understood that very well.

"Yes, my liege. I am ready to carry out your wishes." Ash bowed his head respectfully, turning to face Lucifer, hands clasped behind his back and his feet the standard shoulder length apart. His stance one of rest, and yet always on guard. Trained as a warrior, despite his fleshly reputation and title, Ash was a champion legionnaire. He waited, prepared to carry out Lucifer's command to the best of his ability. Honor and duty would allow nothing less.

"I command you to attend tonight's speed dating at the Cafe. That is an order, Ashmedai."

Well. Shit.

CHAPTER THREE

AN HOUR AND fifteen minutes later, Gabby arrived at her destination. She forked over an exorbitant fee to park her car and was walking through the front door of DeLux Café in no time at all.

Good thing too, as her stomach had started to complain about the lack of food inside of it a good twenty minutes ago. She shivered despite the heat and stood waiting for the hostess to greet her. She was always chilly, no matter the surrounding weather. Her stomach growled again, and she put a hand on her belly as if that would shut the thing up.

"I'm looking for Mariah Bailey Keen," she informed the very pretty hostess, hoping like hell the woman could not hear the incessant gurgling noises.

"Certainly, miss," the woman replied coolly. She glanced at her tablet, raised her eyes to look Gabby over once more before pasting a smile to her face.

Gabby knew what she was thinking. Something along the lines of what was a chubby little nobody doing meeting one of Los Angeles' top realtors for dinner at this hard to get into hotspot.

Well, Gabby had one answer for the female.

Noneya.

As in none of ya beeswax.

Grrr.

Eeek!

Was she actually growling?

She shook her head, pretending she did not just make that horrible noise.

"Are you alright?" The hostess asked.

"Certainly," she replied sweetly.

Too sweetly, in all honesty, but she was trying to keep herself calm. What she really wanted to do was reach out and smack the thin female. *Oh my,* she thought with more than a little trepidation. Maybe a drink or appetizer would put her in a better mood. She'd heard of people getting *hangry*, but this was the first time she understood what they meant.

Easy, Gabs, remember you are a lady.

She sucked in a calming breath, wrinkling her nose at the odd scents she was picking up. There were too many to pin down, so she lifted her hand on the pretense of scratching her nose just to breathe the light perfume she'd spritzed on her wrist before leaving the house. It was a little trick she'd picked up a few months ago when her symptoms had started.

Along with her headaches and stomach cramps, Gabriella had developed a bloodhound's sense of smell. Disconcerting, to say the least. Especially when she'd looked online and read it could indicate some very serious illnesses, including certain types of autoimmune disease and brain tumors.

"I have to tell Mim," she murmured.

"Excuse me?" The hostess glanced back at her, but Gabby just forced a smile and shook her head.

"Nothing," Gabby replied.

The line outside DeLux Cafe was ridiculous for a Wednesday. Gabby glanced out the floor to ceiling windows as they walked, shaking her head at the overdressed would be patrons. There were more designer gowns and jewels outside the restaurant than could be found on a red carpet during awards week.

That was almost nothing compared to the variety within the place. There were people dressed in torn jeans and leather, evening gowns that cost more than her rent back on the East Coast, and almost every state of dress in between. A wild, eclectic mix that made Gabby smile despite feeling like a butterfly on display, with her wings pinned to a corkboard. Everyone was staring. At what, she did not know.

Dear God, tell me they didn't hear my stomach growl too?

This had to be the only town in the world where folks went to expensive restaurants and ordered ridiculously priced hard to pronounce food only to stare at it. Well, Gabby was not one of those people. She enjoyed a wide variety of culinary delights. To eat, not to just look at.

Welcome to LA, she thought, still following the slender young woman through the highly polished café. Leave it to Mim to find a place like this. White tiles gleamed spectacularly, red velvet drapes hung from impossibly high windows, falling in delicate waves all the way to the polished floors. The atmosphere was strange, and the scents, far too many, made Gabby shiver uncomfortably.

People sat in tables, two by two, with odd little black boxes on each one.

Some sort of weird new ordering system, maybe?

She really did not know. There were red and pink paper hearts, balloons, and cherubs floating about or stuck to the walls. Strange décor for an upscale eatery, a bit tacky to be truthful, and by Gabby's calculations, at least a month too early for Valentine's Day. Strange place, she thought amusedly.

Finally, Gabriella spotted Mim with two other gorgeous females sitting at a long table with a sign that read "Sign Up For Speed Dating Here!'.

Uh oh.

Her pulse sped up, and Gabby's heart beat faster.

She didn't.

She couldn't.

Not again!

"Gabs!" Mim shouted before she could turn on her heel and run out of the place.

The two impossibly beautiful women beside her turned to stare at Gabriella and she felt very much like a piece of chocolate in front of two sweets-starved supermodels.

Gulp.

"Don't you run away now, silly." Mim laughed, and the sound was very much like tinkling bells.

Gabriella released a sigh and shook her head. She used to envy her stepmother's beauty. Even though she was not bad looking, cute and chubby as opposed to statuesque and stunning, Gabriella loved the woman too much to let anything come between them.

Even if she was the worst sort of meddler.

"Gabs, let me introduce Eve and Aphrodite." Her stepmother indicated the almost too beautiful to look at brunette and a blonde with a brilliant, perhaps even a little feral, smile on her perfect face. "They are hosting tonight's little get together. Now, I know you said not to interfere, but I thought this would be a great way for you to meet some new people!"

"Uh, nice to meet you, ladies. Excuse us a sec," she said, then turned to face her stepmother. "Mim, what are you doing? I did not sign up for this."

"Honey, look, I went through your laptop, and I saw what you've been googling—"

"What! How could you do that?"

Anger, embarrassment, and fear warred within Gabs as her stepmother admitted to snooping through her things.

Ugh.

She'd thought they'd been through this back in high school. There was a period where Mim looked through everything of Gabby's without permission until finally she had to confront her.

But now, when she could possibly be ill, it felt like the worst kind of betrayal.

"Look, Gabby, I love you like you were my own. Hell, you are my own! And there is no easy way to say this, so I'm just going to break it to you." Mim cleared her throat and grabbed Gabby's elbow with a surprisingly strong grip, hauling her to a quiet corner.

"You aren't dying. Those cramps and headaches, the slight increase in aggression you've been experiencing?

Well, honey, you're experiencing your first *Change*."

"My what? You're telling me I am going through menopause? I'm not even thirty!" She hissed, rubbing her forehead at the sudden sharp pang that went through her.

"No dear, not menopause. This Change is different. You are a Werewolf. A Shifter. Like me and your mother before you. I smelled it on you when you were a pup, but then you didn't Change, and I thought it skipped you. It does that sometimes. Especially back when the Curse was strong."

"I'm cursed too?"

"Yes. No. Hmm." Mim rolled her eyes, tapping a manicured nail against her chin while she gathered her thoughts.

"Well, you see, it was never just you. Besides, no, we are not cursed. Not anymore. All Werewolves used to be bound to the cycles of the moon because of an ancient trespass. It was known as the Curse of St. Natalis, but this spunky little Wolf from New Jersey ended all that and now, dormant Werewolves, such as yourself, are waking up all over the place. Oh honey! I am so proud of you!" Mim gasped and hugged Gabby tight against her.

The woman had always been strong. And she still looked young as ever. She'd never given any indication she was crazy, though. Gabby blinked rapidly.

She should be freaking out. In fact, she should be calling for help. The kind that came with vans and orderlies who carried needles and special little jackets with belts wrapped around them, so the crazy folk didn't hurt themselves or anyone else. And yet, something in the back of Gabby's mind accepted her stepmother's words. It was almost like another voice whispered to her from the dark crevices of her brain.

She's right, Gabby.

We are Wolf.

"Uh, Mim, why don't we sit down here. We can call a doctor—"

"So, is she ready to go? Round one is gonna start up in a bit and without her we're short a girl," Eve stage-whispered, eyeing Gabby, not unkindly. "Are you thinking upstairs or downstairs, Mariah?" The blonde tapped her chin, her pointy teeth catching the lighting from one of the hanging globes overhead as she spoke to Gabby's stepmother.

Gabby's mouth opened and closed like a fish out of water as she tried to comprehend what the heck they were talking about.

Was her stepmom losing it?

Maybe some early form of dementia or psychosis. The tall, statuesque woman couldn't be a Werewolf. And if Mim was one of them, then Gabby, who stood five foot three and outweighed the woman by a good thirty pounds, definitely could not be a... a... whatever the heck she thought she was.

A Wolf.

And yes, you can be one.

In fact, you are.

That husky voice inside Gabriella's

brain whispered once more, causing the woman to let out a short *eeep* that brought Mim's and the other female's eyes directly back to her.

"Uh, round one? Of what?" Gabby asked stupidly.

"Downstairs will be best, I think. Thank you, Eve." Mim stood, nudging Gabby gently in the direction the blonde was leading her.

"I thought we were having dinner."

"Well, dear, I promised your father I would take care of you, and I am," Mim said as she managed to half push, half drag Gabby to the stop of a long, winding staircase that led somewhere below the DeLux Café. "You might not believe it, sweetheart, but this is for your own good."

"But you just told me I'm a Werewolf," Gabby hissed quietly as more people shoved past them to get down the stairs. "And now you want me to go speed dating?"

"Yes. It will be good for you. You need to get out. I know you are a goody goody, Gabriella Keen, but your Wolf is coming on fast and you'll need help. Nothing better than a romance to get the old supernatural blood pumping! Cha chow." Mim winked, and Gabby cringed.

Why did old people not know they were old?

She wondered as she felt someone tug on her hand. Gabby had no choice but to follow, barely making out bouncy brown hair and a killer figure.

Oh, it was Aphrodite.

CHAPTER FOUR

THE APHRODITE?

Nah.

But she is gorgeous.

And that body.

Holy moly!

"It's me alright," the beauty replied with a wink. "And thanks for the compliment, but I understood you liked men?"

"Huh? Oh, yeah, I do. I mean, I think I do—"

How could she answer a question like that to the Goddess of Love herself?

Even more troubling was the fact she was even considering this to be real.

Was Gabby really buying into all this?

She shook her head, feeling confused and a little overwhelmed.

"There are strict rules for the speed dating. No touching, licking, kissing, biting, basically nothing ending in *ing* unless you or your date is invited to and permitted to do so, of course," Aphrodite said with a sly wink, looking back over her shoulder at Gabby.

How she navigated the stairs in her lethally high stilettos was beyond the shorter, rounder woman who was struggling to keep up.

Speed dating.

Her?

What was Mim thinking?

It was almost as unbelievable to conceive of as the notion that she, Gabriella Keen, Sunday school teacher and all around goody two shoes, was a Werewolf.

You are a Wolf.

Grrr.

She stopped midstep and closed her eyes, trying to get her growling bits, as in her Wolf and her stomach both, to shut the flub up.

Sigh.

She really needed to start cursing. But dang it, she just couldn't. The f word turned into all sorts of silly things like *funk*, *flub*, *flap*, and *furp*. The s word often became *shoot*, the b word stopped at *bit*, and so on.

"Gabby, right? Look, dear, the rest is all easy to follow. You sit, drink, chat, sniff, see if you click. And if you don't, just move on when the timer dings."

"Wait, what? Sniff? Ding? Huh?" Gabby's eyebrows disappeared into her hairline. She inhaled a breath, then another, trying not to hyperventilate with this new and sudden influx of information.

"I'm sorry, I meant no offence," Aphrodite replied, looking properly chided. Heck. This woman had pouting down to an art.

"I tend to forget my manners

sometimes, but honestly, Wolves and other Shifters tend to sniff out their mates. Something about the Fates lacing their pheromones with something that triggers awareness when their destined mate is near."

"Look, I don't know what is happening here. Is this real? Was Mim serious? And are you really leading me to some underground speed dating thing?"

"Honey, I gather you haven't *changed* yet, is that right?"

"But I did change my dress—"

"Not your dress," Aphrodite whispered, taking her by the arm and pulling her down the last few steps.

She stopped her just on the other side of the polished staircase, in a dark secluded corner. Gabriella was breathing heavily. There were too many fragrances assaulting her senses, and her stomach tightened as she started to panic, albeit mildly.

"Look at me, Gabriella," Aphrodite commanded. "I am sure Mariah meant well, throwing you in the deep end like this, but I have one question for you before you begin."

Gabby nodded, willing the woman to just get on with it already.

What did she want to know?

Did insanity run in the family?

Had she gotten her flea shots?

Was she gonna potty on the floor?

Chew on the chairs?

What, dang it, what?!

"Are you a virgin?"

Well, that wasn't what she'd expected. Gabby stopped hyperventilating and straightened her shoulders. Her cheeks burned, and she knew they'd be a dusky, unflattering shade of pink that clashed with the red lights of the room they were now in.

"Hey, I may not look like you, oh Goddess of love, but I have been in love. At least, I thought I'd been. And the answer is no, I am not a virgin."

"Great! I was worried for a minute. Follow me," Aphrodite replied with an even wider grin than before. "Welcome," she said, indicating the room before her, "to Speed Dating With the Denizens of the Underworld!"

Gabriella's eyes popped out of her head.

ASH

What in the world?

But she knew as she gazed at the men and women, creatures really, sitting at tables, some with enormous wings, protruding fangs, tails, claws, and glowing eyes, that she wasn't in the world anymore. Not her world, at any rate.

"When you say Underworld, is that figuratively or literally?" Gabby asked while Eve sauntered over to greet them, a piece of paper in her hand.

"Here's your ballot. Did I spell your name right?" she asked, ignoring Gabby's question.

"Yep." Gabby nodded, only half listening.

"This is the Underworld Café, dear," Aphrodite stated calmly, leading her to a table where a man with green-tinted skin sat nervously.

"Hello everyone, it's Wednesday and you know what that means!" The beautiful Goddess began laying out the rules while Eve unceremoniously shoved Gabby into the chair.

She gulped, took the drink Eve proffered. It was a swirling concoction that dazzled the eye with red sugar crystals around the rim and golden swirls inside.

"Begin!"

Gulp.

CHAPTER FIVE

ASH GROWLED IMPATIENTLY and sunk into his assigned seat. He had more important business to attend than this, for fuck's sake. Creed, one of his legates, had reported some more unsavory activity at the southwest border. He ordered double the guard to check it out and was waiting impatiently for the report.

Fucking hell.

He would've gone himself if this hadn't been a direct order from Lucifer.

Who would have ever thought the Demon of Lust could sink so low?

He was Asmodeus. The Ashmedai! A Prince of Hell. General of the Daemonium Guard. A fucking legend in the Underworld. Conquests by the thousand.

Who knew more about lovemaking and the art of seduction than he?

Him! Ordered to attend this speed dating event like somebody's ugly step-cousin. Bah! If the Lord of the Underworld wanted him to get laid, he supposed he had no choice. So, which of these all too willing females was he going to go home with?

So many there reeking of lust and desire. He felt their eyes weighing and measuring him. Heard their whispered gasps of surprise that the Demon of Lust was there, in the flesh.

Ugh.

His boredom bordered on disdain for the throngs of females. He even snarled at one who dared step too close. Truth was, none there appealed to him.

He frowned, his thoughts turning grim as he tried not to look too closely at any one person there. He simply was not ready for dating. Fucking was another story. His body was in fine working order. Sex without emotion had always been one of his specialties. But not even that stirred his appetites.

Not after all he'd been through. Yes, he realized he sounded like a whiny fucking human.

But so what?

Maybe they had it right when they promoted sharing each other's feelings and emotional awareness.

He was a Demon, true, but he still had a soul, for fuck's sake.

Besides, what help did he need finding a female?

He huffed and readjusted his specialty tailored jacket. It was quite fine and superbly cut, if he said so himself.

Thanks to Arachne, of course, and her custom clothing boutique, *Metamorphosis*. That was one highlight of the new Underworld Ash was rather fond of. No one cut a suit like the female

Spider Shifter. And the fact her silk was imbued with magical elements that allowed for him to reveal wings and tail without damage was just a bonus.

He wore her latest design tonight, admiring the feel of the slate colored suit. Lucifer had commanded he dress to the occasion, and after all that time spent in rags, imprisoned by the foulest of the foul, Ash did not mind donning some finery. Indeed, some things about being home were almost too good to be true.

He still felt unsettled, but at least he was back among friends. In his own house, and with so many lovely luxuries. His callused fingers brushed against the smooth silk of his shirt, and Ash silently thanked Arachne's efforts. Her new boutique was exquisite and she had a knack for utilizing her clients' desires, such as his own taste for finery in her creations, surpassing his expectations in her execution. Lust encompassed many things, including an affinity for all things beautiful.

Speaking of which, he ducked his head when a certain familiar blonde headed his way.

Shit.

He had hoped to go on unnoticed, but alas, that was not to pass. Hands on her hips and one eyebrow raised, Eve hunted him across the room.

"Well, I knew you'd been summoned, Asmodeus, but I did not expect to see you here," Eve said with her familiar, and always annoying, smirk.

The Vampire female had been after him to attend this little soiree since he'd returned. Eve and Aphrodite had concocted this plan to match up citizens of the Underworld with their fated mates. Even destiny fucked up occasionally, and sometimes mates somehow eluded one another during their actual lifetimes.

What fucking ever.

Ash had never lived as anything other than a Demon. He was not dead or undead. He simply was. His existence was not like others. Yes, he could die, he supposed, but where he would end up was anyone's guess.

Born in Hell, returning there would be like going home, wouldn't it?

And he did so prefer Purgatory for the

time being.

"Well, ready to admit I was right?" Eve asked.

"You? Ha! I was ordered to attend, and I would never defy Lucifer," he replied blandly.

"Oh." Eve frowned. "Well, since you are here, I hope you will have an open mind about finding your mate—"

"I don't think so, Eve. And I apologize if I am rude, years away from civilization can do that to a Demon, but I have absolutely no interest in being here. I am only sitting at this ridiculously decorated table because, like I said, I was ordered to do so."

"Drat! I told Aphrodite the confetti and glitter were just too much," she murmured, brushing some of the paper hearts off of his table and into her manicured hands.

"Eve, relax. I will give Lucifer a good report on your scheme here."

"It's not a scheme! We really can help you find your soul mate, Ash!"

"Eve, some of us simply do not have soul mates. It is fine. I am okay with being alone—"

"That's crazy talk! Look, the Fates wouldn't have done that to you, Ash. Everyone has a mate. Everyone," Eve replied sternly.

"Fine, Eve. Whatever you say." Ash nodded, refusing to argue the matter.

He turned away from the sympathy on her face, missing the ambitious gleam in her bright eyes. He picked up the drink he'd ordered from a passing server, a tumbler of *Bitter Bite*, an artisan whiskey distilled in Maccon City by a Werewolf with a knack for spirits. He drank his neat, rolling the liquid in his mouth as he absorbed the subtle lavender and orange notes.

Music played in the background, but he hardly recognized it. Eve had left him alone, thank the gods, but truth was he kind of felt isolated. He paid little mind to those casting curious glances his way. He had a certain reputation, and those who knew him were perhaps wondering what he was doing there.

They'd probably laugh if he told them he was wondering the same thing.

Why couldn't Lucifer just let him go off on a tour with one of his legions?

Maybe a few months battling the

soulless ones would be good for him.

Take his mind off his own shit. It would be like therapy!

And that was seen as a good thing these days, wasn't it?

Ugh.

He moved in his seat restlessly. If only he could wear his wings and horns, but he'd tucked them away for safety's sake. He did not need anyone with beer muscles picking a fight with a Demon of his rank.

This was going to suck. Ash had no delusions that Eve was right about him finding his mate at a speed dating party. But he was a soldier first, and he'd follow orders.

Still, that didn't mean he was prepared when Aphrodite sounded the call to begin. Before he knew it, Ash was politely declining room keys and phone numbers from half a dozen women and one man. There were people and other beings, in all shapes, sizes, and species. But no one caught his eye. Not even for a quickie.

And wasn't that disappointing?

He'd assumed he'd find at least a bed partner for the night for all his efforts.

Ugh.

How droll.

The room was abuzz with potential, something he was able to discern in the varying scents. It appealed to his Demon side. After all, identifying desires was Ash's angle. It was how he'd operated for millennia. And yet, he could not even fake interest in any single person there.

He was just not interested in the smiling, overly perfumed denizens. All of whom seemed to say the exact same thing. Without fail. Every time the buzzer rang, and he was forced to rise and swap seats, Ash cringed at the usual introductions.

Hi, my name is blah blah. I like blah blah. And I am looking for blah blah blah.

What did he care what any of them were looking for?

He glanced over at where Aphrodite and Eve were conversing. Heads together, they looked over some sort of electronic tablet pointing and focusing like a pair of generals plotting out a war. He just shook his head.

Love really is a battlefield, he mused.

But he had nothing to worry about on

that front. After the vicious mind warp Molloch had put him through, Ash was positive he wouldn't know love if it bit him on the ass.

Buzzzzzzz!

He stood, nodding politely at the woman he'd just ignored for the past five minutes, and sat down at the next table. Inhaling, he took his seat, almost falling off the thing, when a sudden wave of uncontrollable desire hit him square in the gut.

"Hi." A shy voice reached his ears, but he was still too caught up in that crazy, delicious scent.

Bright raspberries with a hint of lime zest, colorful and enticing. Just the sort of thing he would love to imbibe on any occasion. Beneath that was a more complex assortment of flavors. Vanilla bean, lavender, and oak.

Fucking hell.

He didn't want to move, didn't want to open his eyes, simply wanted to sit and breathe her in. It was a her. Woman. He was quite certain. That depth of fragrance could only come from a female.

Human or supernatural?

That was harder to distinguish.

Ash took another breath, ignoring the nervous clearing of the woman's throat. But he could not put it off any longer. Much as he would have liked to simply sit in silence and breathe, he only had a small amount of time with the woman. And the clock was ticking. Stealing himself against disappointment, Ash

ASH

opened his eyes.

Holy fuck.

"Who are you?"

The words slipped from his tongue without his permission. Stunned, he found himself waiting for an answer rather impatiently. Never had a woman held his attention so. She had big blue eyes, like cornflowers, warm chestnut hair with golden highlights, and a charming rosy glow that made him ache all over just to look at her.

Her figure, though she was sitting, was rounded perfection. She positively glowed there, in the dark, and his body reacted violently. Thank fuck for Arachne's weaving or his cock would've torn a seam! That's how hard he got, and in an instant too!

Curious.

"Oh, why bother with names. Just color me fascinated," the vibrant woman said with a shake of her head and a small giggle.

That was when Ash noted the number of empty glasses on her table. Raising his eyebrows, he lifted one, sniffed and closed his eyes. There was enough alcohol in one cup to knock a normal on her ass, which, with another sniff, he concurred she was not. No, definitely not entirely human.

Shifter maybe?

Still, this was quite odd.

"So, what are you? An Elf? Jackalope? Angel, maybe? You sure are pretty enough to be," she murmured.

"Uh, thanks, I think. Do you come

here often?" he asked, hating the cliché, but he wanted to know more about her.

"Who me? No!" She laughed again. "I'm just a schoolteacher. Well, that's not entirely true, You see, this morning I woke up believing I was just a teacher, Sunday school, actually. Then my stepmother told me I was something more and signed me up for whatever this is."

"Something more?"

"Yep. Anyway, it hasn't happened yet, so I am thinking Mim's just a little bit nuts, then she went and introduced me to like the *Eve* and *Aphrodite*."

"That must have been shocking."

"Totally! But despite being ridiculously gorgeous, they were quite nice to me. They showed me around the place, explained the whole speed dating thing, and okay, I mean, I thought they were nuts."

"As anyone rational would," Ash replied with a grin.

She was dazzling him with her childlike enthusiasm and utter enjoyment. She seemed to be having the time of her life. Odd, considering she was entirely new to the supernatural world from what she was telling him.

"Right? But then they gave me these drinks, and so far, so good. I mean, I met a couple of men who claimed they can turn into Bears and Dragons. I mean, they sure were big! And, ooh, I even met a guy who says he's a Jersey Devil," she said without taking a breath.

Ash's head was spinning, but

whether that was from her fast talking or the intoxicating fragrance wafting off her, he didn't know. He wanted to sit there and listen to her forever. But he also wanted to hunt down every male who'd spoken to her before he did.

"So, out of those Bears and Dragons, anyone take your fancy?" he could not help but ask. Nerves on edge, he waited while she swallowed more of her beverage from a straw, causing her lips to pucker most enticingly, before she shook her head no.

"Mmm mm. So far, you're the only one who didn't just sit here and sniff at me. Is that like a thing? Cause it's super weird. Hey, how many calories are in these things?" she asked, picking up her hand and waving the server over for another round.

Uh oh.

Ash grimaced. No wonder she was talking a mile a minute. The glasses littering the table were all empty, having been previously full of one of Aphrodite and Eve's special mixed drinks.

Fucking hell.

The Goddess of Love was renowned for her ability to knock a person on his or her ass with one of her cocktails. Aphrodite! He silently cursed the Goddess when the small, luscious female who made him long for things he'd never dared before stood up. She swayed on her feet, adorably tiny ones encased in low heels with a sling back that made his mouth water.

"Easy now," Ash muttered, standing

in time to take gentle hold of her elbows. "Steady on."

"Thanks. I, um, need the little girls' room," she mumbled, and Ash nodded, without letting go. Her skin was soft and warm beneath his fingers. He quite liked it and had no plans to relinquish his hold until she spoke again.

"I need my arm back first, though." The gorgeous stranger laughed, smiling up at him with big blue eyes that sparkled in the dim light, and fuck him, Ash couldn't breathe.

"Beautiful," he whispered.

"Gabby," she corrected, gathering her purse before walking away.

"Gabby?"

"Yep. Gabriella Keen." She hiccupped.

He stared, enthralled. She was so

adorable. So full of promise. Ash should walk away now, quick before he tainted her with his past. But instead of saying goodbye, his next words surprised him.

"Lovely to meet you, Gabriella. Please allow me to escort you."

"To the potty?" She cocked her head to the side, causing one honey colored curl to land in the lovely crevice between her bountiful breasts.

Ash swallowed, then hissed.

Actually fucking hissed.

Out loud.

His cock strained against his pants. He hadn't felt this out of control since he'd hit Demonic puberty about two thousand years ago.

Holy fuck.

Even more astounding was the fact

the curvy little minx seemed completely unaware of the affect she had on him. He could easily pick up on sexual mind games and flirtatious teasing, but she was doing neither. At least, not on purpose. Maybe that was why he was so unwilling to say his farewells.

Gabriella was like a breath of fresh air in the typically sulfuric Underworld. He wanted to continue their conversation. Hell, he'd listen to her read the phone book if she wanted. So yeah. If she needed to use the facilities, hell yeah, he'd escort her. If she wanted to go dancing, find a restaurant, go for a walk, or fuck it, fly to the moon, Ash was her guy.

Or he would be.

Soon.

Grrr.

"I'll take you anywhere you want to go," Ash replied, voice deep and gravelly. He swallowed his next growl, not wanting to scare the female. But she merely grinned, tilting her head back, stepping closer, and steadying herself with a hand on his chest.

"No one has ever said that to me before, uh, I don't know your name," Gabriella replied with a wide, and not entirely sober, smile.

"I'm Ash."

"Ash? I like that. It's unusual. Well then, Ash, I guess you can walk me to the restroom."

Ash growled, pleasure filling him at the sound of his name on her plump lips. He wanted nothing more than to grab and pull her closer, flush against his hardened body, just so he could breathe her in and savor her warmth.

She tormented his senses with her nearness. A good kind of torture. The type that made him want her all the more. Still, she did not give in to blatant flirtation or coquettish displays. She simply was that alluring.

To be honest, it was a tad disappointing.

Did he want more than he was wanted?

Did he completely lose his touch?

What if Gabriella did not find him attractive?

He frowned.

Impossible!

Ash held out his arm, unwilling to let

her wander out of his sight. His Demonic side relaxing slightly when she placed her small, warm hard on his sleeve.

"Awww, how chivalrous!" she exclaimed, clapping her hands, wobbling a bit more before she clasped onto his arm.

The second she touched him, Ash tingled all over. He felt as if he was all aflame. He did not speak. Couldn't utter a syllable. So, he simply walked, navigating them through the crowded bar, growling at more than one patron for not moving out of their way fast enough. Soon, he'd cleared a path to the ladies' room and held the door while the lovely and slightly tipsy Gabriella walked inside.

"Be right back," she smiled, reaching

up and tapping his lips with her finger.

Ash took the opportunity to steal a kiss, pressing his lips to the warm delicate digit. The moment his skin connected with hers, Ash knew something was different.

Strange.

Special.

All the above.

The room seemed to turn red. Or maybe that was just his vision. His heart thundered. That under-used muscle beat a furious tattoo inside of his chest. Without his meaning them to, his horns, wings, and tail all made an appearance. Forcing their way through the delicate fabric of his suit, but what the fuck did he care? Arachne had designed it for just that purpose.

"Uh, Ash?" Aphrodite approached him cautiously. "Ash!" she yelled, gaining his attention. Not entirely a good thing, since his lips peeled back while he snarled at her.

"Ah, she is yours, then?"

The Goddess of love was wise not to smirk, but Ash had no reply. He was still not capable of speech.

Was the Goddess correct?

Could Gabriella Keen be his one?

His fated mate.

No way.

She couldn't be.

But the voice inside of him, his Demon voice, had only one word to say in response.

Mine.

CHAPTER SIX

GABRIELLA WASHED HER hands in the sink, wondering how the heck people could see what they were doing in the dark reddish glow of what passed for lighting in this club.

"We're mostly able to see in the dark," a voice said to her left, and Gabby whipped around to see the beautiful brunette Goddess had found her once more.

"Can you read my mind?"

"You were talking out loud, actually," Aphrodite returned.

"I was? Ooops!" Gabby giggled.

"How many of those drinks have you had, dear?"

"I don't know. Why? Ooof." Gabriella turned to face the impossibly beautiful Goddess only to collide with the wall.

Thank goodness for boobs!

She let loose another giggle. Her double D's hit the tiled wall first, causing her to bounce back. She bumped into the Goddess who was thin and tall, but somehow stood her ground against the much rounder female.

"Whoopsie! Hey Goddess person? Um,

I think I'm drunk," she muttered before bursting into chuckles. *Ha ha ha!* First time for everything."

"You've never been drunk?"

"Nope."

"Oh dear." Aphrodite frowned, grabbing onto her arm before she could slide to the floor. "Your metabolism should burn off the alcohol faster than this, but perhaps it's slow because you've never Shifted. Hmm, tell you what," Aphrodite said. "There's a man waiting for you outside. A Demon. Real good guy. Anyway, he'll take care of you—"

"You want to send me off with some strange man, or sort of man? What is he anyway, a Goblin? Gnome? Donkey Shifter? Hey, wait a sec! Isn't that like a recipe for date rape?"

"What? No. No! OMG! Gabby!" Aphrodite released Gabby's arm, and this time she slipped all the way to the floor.

The Goddess hissed and covered her eyes with her perfectly manicured nails. At least they looked manicured, Gabby couldn't exactly tell from her position on the floor.

"I would never do anything like that," Aphrodite said through clenched teeth. "But here's the deal, love, you are wasted. Completely fucked up. Get it? Now, yes, Ash is a Demon. But he is also the only person here I would actually trust to see you safely home. He can't hurt you. He won't."

"Fine, fine. I need some air," Gabby

said, getting to her feet slowly.

***

"Is she alright?" Ash looked frantically from the Goddess to Gabriella and back again.

"Yes," Aphrodite explained, holding firmly onto her elbow before finally shoving her toward him.

Gabby had to admit he was handsome. In fact, she rather liked when he looked at her. As he was doing right then, with eyes that were positively obsidian.

"Gabriella," he breathed her name.

"You know my name."

"Aphrodite told me," he replied, brushing her hair off her forehead. "Come, let's get some air, sweet."

Then he was leading her outside, and Gabby, despite every after school special she'd ever watched, and all her Sunday school lessons, went with him.

Imagine that.

A goody two shoes and a Demon.

He wrapped one arm around her waist, holding her up firmly, and she was more than grateful for the support. Her body felt numb, achy too. She wondered if that happened to everyone when they drank, whatever that was she'd been drinking.

"So, you're a Werewolf?" Ash asked.

"Who me? Uh, yeah. I suppose. Did I tell you that?"

"No," he replied. "Is it true you just learned about this tonight?"

"Yeah, my Mim told me."

"Mim?"

"My stepmom. I called her Mim growing up," Gabby said, leaning on him.

"I see." He spoke to her in a low, charming voice with an accent she could not quite place.

Not quite British, but not American. Like European, but different. She wanted to hear him speak more, wanted him to say her name.

Suddenly, she felt warm. Very, very warm. Like flames dancing along her skin, caressing, almost kissing her. Then she gasped. What had started as light tickling was now full blown fire.

"Are you alright?"

"I feel hot," she said just as a cramp hit her.

ASH

Ash opened a door, and suddenly, wings sprouted from his back. Along with a tail and horns. She knew they should frighten her, but she couldn't focus on anything other than the pain.

"Hang on," the Demon growled.

Ash scooped her up in his arms, his handsome face stern, and if she wasn't mistaken, worried. Cool air met her skin as he flew with her through the doors of the bar. Holy crap. She was flying. Darn it! And she couldn't even enjoy it!

"Easy," he whispered, as he lowered to what looked like a courtyard.

She could not tell, but she knew they weren't in LA anymore. The sky was a strange shade of purple and red. And there were other creatures flying about, some with feathered wings, others with batlike ones not unlike Ash's, but not nearly as impressive.

"Boss! You're home! Let me aid you!"

A small man, at least, she thought he was a man, came running out to greet them. He moved strangely, in a sort of side scramble like a crab. In fact, he had crablike claws instead of legs on his lower body. Ash growled, and the creature stopped dead in his tracks.

"Sorry for growling at you, Ernie. But it's okay. I've got her. You may retire for the evening," Ash spoke to the cre—, er, to Ernie.

"Thank you, *boss*," Ernie mumbled, casting an angry glance at Gabby before crawling away.

"Who's that?" she asked, her head still spinning.

"Who, not what?" Ash asked, eyebrows raised, and she could tell he was teasing her.

"Well, since I am dreaming all this up, I don't suppose it matters. Tell me both."

"You're not dreaming, sweet. And that was Ernie. He works for me. He is an *Imp*."

"Are you sure I am not dreaming?" Gabriella asked, laying her head on his chest. It was still much too foggy to hold up on her own. This must be why she'd never indulged so heavily before.

Ugh.

Why did people even like drinking if this was the result?

"Why must you be dreaming, sweet?"

"Well, let's see, tonight I was told I am

a Werewolf. My stepmom signed me up to meet a guy through a supernatural speed dating service. I got drunk for the first time on who knows what mixed cocktail Eve, *the actual Eve by the way*, and Aphrodite, *aka Goddess of Love*, whipped up for me."

"I see."

"That's not all," she continued. "Most recently, I am being carried all over the place by this ridiculously cute guy, who is not gasping for air even though I weigh a ton, and I am pretty sure he can fly. Seriously, how drunk am I? Did you really have wings on your back a minute ago?" Gabby frowned, looking at the space those large black appendages had appeared only moments ago.

"First, you are light as a feather.

Perfect, in fact. Second, my wings are still there," he explained, causing all sorts of delicious waves of warmth to run up and down her spine. "You just can't see them."

"Wait. What? Where did they go?"

"When I need them, they will appear. You see, they are simply existing in another plane of reality."

"Oh." Gabriella sighed, nodding against his chest.

***

The fact the sumptuous mortal was taking him at his word was surprising in and of itself. That she trusted him with her person was something else entirely. Yes, he was the Demon of Lust, but he had caused enough death and destruction to have forged quite the reputation for being fearsome. And yet, one brush of her hands over his chest, one sigh and the feel of her warm breath on his neck, and Asmodeus, the Demon of Lust, a Prince of Hell, and General of the Daemonium Guard, was undone.

Mine.

His Demonic side whispered in his mind, and he felt the truth of it to his core. Yes. She was his.

But was he worthy to claim her?

Before his doubts could grab hold of him, twisting and turning him inside out until he ran screaming from the place, his sweet would be mate touched his cheek.

"You really are so handsome," she murmured, and her cornflower blue eyes widened as her fingertips ran over his lips.

Grrr.

Ash growled low in his chest. His body trembled at her tentative touch. Slowly, gently, he placed her down on a plush leather sofa before turning away. He had to and fast. Need and desire burned through him like wildfire. He wanted her so damn badly.

Instead of giving in to that lust, he turned to grab her a bottle of cold spring water. Ash helped Gabby kick off her shoes, realizing the female might think it rude, but she seemed weak and out of sorts, and he wanted her comfortable.

"Has the cramping stopped?"

"Yes, but I am dying of thirst," she replied, tucking her feet beneath her and grabbing the bottle he held out to her. Ash watched with concern while she guzzled the cool liquid, hoping it refreshed her.

"Better?" he asked.

"Oh yes," she said after finishing every drop.

"Thanks, I guess I needed that."

"Not used to drinking?"

"Who me? I'm a Sunday school teacher. I don't drink. I don't smoke—"

"You don't leave bars with strange men?" He grinned, liking the blush that crept across her cheeks.

He watched as her eyes regained focus. The fogginess in her head seemed to have retreated. At least, she no longer appeared drunk to him. He suspected he knew what happened.

"I feel strange. Like I was drunk a moment ago, and now, well, I feel better," she stated, shaking her head, perhaps in disbelief.

He could only imagine how she felt. Getting used to supernatural metabolism must be difficult for one raised as only human. Concern rose inside of him once more, surprising him, but not really. His entire being seemed attuned to the lovely female.

"You feel like your entire system went into overdrive?"

"Yes!"

"I believe I can explain. You see, your Wolf side is trying to burn through the unfamiliar alcohol in your bloodstream."

"My Wolf side? Oh, right, I told you about that," she mumbled.

"You did. And it is nothing to be embarrassed about."

"Are you sure about that? I mean, what happens when I get furry? Will I run around sniffing people's butts?"

"I suspect that is not accurate," Ash replied with a grin. His heart squeezed inside his chest at her remarkable vulnerability.

Had a woman ever discussed butt sniffing with him before and managed to still look absolutely adorable?

Not to his immediate recollection.

"You know, I can't tell if I am suddenly oversharing or if everyone here can read minds," she replied with a self-deprecating laugh.

"I imagine it is overwhelming," he said sympathetically. "Finding out you're a

Werewolf. Meeting a bunch of supernaturals in a bar in the Underworld."

"Flying through the sky in the arms of some strange man?"

"Yeah, that too," he murmured, noting her pale cheeks turning a pretty, dusky shade of pink.

This time, they both laughed. It felt so real, so right, to be able to simply sit and talk with her. It was strange for him. Demons did not usually get all touchy feely. When he was in pursuit of a female, he typically used all his powers of seduction to get what he wanted.

But what did he want?

What really?

The question startled him almost as much as the answer. His inner Demon seemed to know before he did.

Ash wanted her.

Wholly and completely.

Mate.

"Yeah," she said, clearing her throat and recapturing his attention. "So, where are we?"

"My home," he replied immediately, wanting more than ever to put her at ease.

He watched as she looked around and saw the rather plain interior. It wasn't that it was bare or even cheap, on the contrary, but it was impersonal. Something that made him feel a little jittery.

"I know it is not much—"

"Are you kidding? I was raised with Mim's tastes. I know quality, and this place is that. The bones of this house are sublime, and the furniture is really nice, Ash."

"Thank you," he said automatically, but he knew it seemed sterile and empty.

"How long have you lived here?"

"It's been mine a long time," he explained. "Demons live a lot longer than most. But, um, I've been gone a while."

"Oh," she replied, squeezing his hand.

He hated to think what she thought of anyone living in such an impersonal space.

Did she find him shallow?

Or reticent?

He was neither, truly.

But how was he going to convey that and convince her how much she meant to him?

"What is it?" Ash asked when she started to bite her lower lip. He reached out and smoothed the abused flesh from her teeth, concern filling every inch of him.

"Oh, nothing." Her face was flaming, and he knew she was embarrassed at being caught scrutinizing his home.

"You live here alone?"

"Yes. Well, except for Ernie and the other Imps in my employ. I have owned this place for centuries," he murmured.

"You said you were gone a while. Gone where?"

"It's not something I like to talk about," he said.

"I'm so sorry to pry," Gabby said, and he immediately regretted his hasty words.

"No! I mean, I should apologize. This is not easy to explain," he said and exhaled, trying to steady his nerves. "I played a minor role in the recent Werewolf uprising, you see."

"Werewolf uprising?"

"Yes," he said, stilling when she took his hand. "I know you are new to this, so your stepmother would not have had the chance to explain. A few years ago, a young Wolf named Grazi Kelly ended the Curse of St. Natalis that had doomed all Werewolves to only shift during the full moon."

"Wow, that sounds terrible."

"You don't know the half of it, sweet, and for that I am glad. But you see, my part in it was not good. I was captured and bound to serve an evil Demon for the past hundred years or so. After he was defeated by Grazi and Lucifer, really, I was freed. That was fairly recently," he said, rushing through his explanation and amazed at how light he felt afterward.

"That must have been awful," Gabby whispered, both hands holding his. Her blue eyes filled with unshed tears and his heart squeezed at her obvious concern.

"It was. I'm sorry," Ash began. "I've monopolized the conversation. Tell me, how are you feeling? Need more water?"

Gabriella shook her head. He was being evasive, and he knew it.

But could anyone blame him?

He did not want his future mate to

see him as a monster or some weirdo.

Would she judge him for his past?

Maybe.

But for some reason, it was a risk he had to take. Ash did not want her to go into this thing blindly. If she was going to stay, it would be with her eyes open.

"Do you go to that speed dating thing often?" Gabby asked, sidetracking him.

"No," he said, looking away and shaking his head. "Uh, actually, I had planned on never going, but I am glad I did, Gabriella Keen."

"Oh, um, I am sorry to have dragged you away from it—"

"No point in staying anymore, was there?"

"How do you mean?" Gabriella asked, her voice a soft whisper like the sweet caress of silk against bare skin.

His inner Demon growled, wanting him to move closer to the female, but Ash hesitated. She seemed truly curious. But why would a beautiful woman, er, Wolf, want anything to do with him?

"Ash," she said, a ghost of a smile playing at the corner of her mouth. "Why are you looking at me like that?"

"Like what?"

"Like you don't know whether to kiss me or run screaming?"

She tried to play it off like it was a joke, but he knew she meant it.

Was he sending mixed signals?

Perhaps.

Either way, it was time to clear the air. Ash never backed down from a battle, and what else was the path to true love? He sucked in a breath, taking a moment to enjoy her raspberry lime vanilla essence before he put himself on the firing line.

"Tell me first, Gabriella, what do you know about mates?"

"Mates? Isn't that like Australian for friends?"

"Yes, but that is not what I mean," he said, trying hard not to laugh. Hell, he'd never laughed so much in his very long life as he had with her.

"Explain it to me, Ash."

CHAPTER SEVEN

"YOU KNOW, YOU'RE unlike anyone I've ever met, Gabriella Keen," Ash whispered.

"How's that?"

"Where would I even begin," he replied. "First, back to mates. You see, sweet, in the supernatural world some beings are destined, chosen by the

Fates, sometimes the universe itself, to be together. We call them fated mates."

"That's a beautiful story," she said, not daring for a second to believe what she secretly hoped he was saying.

"It is more than story," he replied. "One that I never dared hope for myself, but you see, I think it must be true because here you are."

The way he gazed at her, looking her right in the eyes, told her he was being truthful. Gabby licked her suddenly dry lips. She'd never had much luck with men. Always settled for whatever she thought she could get and tried to make the best. But here was a guy, *a ridiculously gorgeous guy*, looking at her like she was a warm, gooey chocolate chip cookie on a cold day.

She swallowed. Heat blossomed in her belly, moving upward and out, through her veins, to every nerve ending. But what she was feeling was so much more than a carnal response to his overwhelming masculinity. Her heart was pounding like she'd just run a marathon. All throughout his speech, a voice seemed to whisper in the back of her mind.

Mate, the voice said.

Mine.

Gabby had been kissed before. Heck, she'd even had sex. But she never felt this way with any other person in her whole life. Like her entire body was on fire, watching and waiting for him to do, well, anything.

Holy cow.

ASH

Was this what desire felt like?

She moved forward in her seat, closer to him. It was as if she were drawn to Ash by some powerful, invisible force. Ash licked his lips, his whole body so very still he could've been stone.

Was she an idiot?

Of course, he did not reciprocate her feelings. She was a dowdy little schoolteacher, and he, well, he was this powerful, devilishly handsome Demon.

What could she possibly offer him?

Mate.

"So, uh, I take it every Judeo-Christian tradition I'd been taught to believe is completely made up? As a Sunday school teacher, this is somewhat troubling," she said, going with the first thing that popped into her head.

Ash frowned. He seemed to consider her question before his response.

"Well, that all depends," he said. "There are infinite planes of reality in the multiverse, Gabriella. Different creeds, belief systems, and traditions do have something to do with that. You see, it has been my experience, the more you believe in something, the more life you give it. Understand?"

"But you are a Demon, right?"

"Yes," he replied slowly, almost hissing the word.

She saw his impossibly wide shoulders tense and took a moment to study his impressive physique. He looked like an Olympian, a God, a Warrior, a Demon, she supposed. With all the prowess, strength, and beauty of a professional athlete, and then some. Yes, he was more. Like his extreme good looks were somehow enhanced simply by his being whatever it is he really was.

Demon, her mind seemed to whisper.

Mate.

Once more, Gabby marveled at how totally unafraid she was. Ash was potent, dynamic, alluring, all the above.

But a Demon?

What self-respecting Catholic raised girl would ever give in to her desires with a Demon?

This one right here, her inner voice shouted.

That's when she finally made up her mind. Regardless of species, subspecies, creed, or whatever, Gabriella was ready to admit she wanted Ash.

He might be a Demon, but so what?

She was a Werewolf if Mim was to be believed.

Wolf.

Yes.

She shook her head, willing that inner voice to hush now. She was coming on to something big, huge, a monumental crossroads in her life. This *goody goody* was about to do something *very, very* bad. And it wasn't because of any supernatural mixed drink, thank Eve and Aphrodite very much.

"You're not evil," Gabby stated, getting ready to do what she wanted.

"How do you know that?" Ash replied, his pale skin and chiseled good looks so appealing in the dim light of the living room, she could've cried.

"Because." She shrugged, deciding then to fully embrace the incredible circumstances she found herself in.

Gabby moved into his personal space, building her courage as she did. Then she did something that a day ago would have been unthinkable to the curvy little schoolteacher.

She reached out, smoothing her hands across his hard chest, up and around, linking her arms around his thick neck. Gabby pressed herself close to his warm body, so close she could feel his soft breath on her face.

"If you were evil, I wouldn't want to do this," she whispered, breathing in the uniquely spicy masculine scent of him.

The flames of desire licked at her skin until she trembled with it. Then she kissed him. And for the first time in her life, little Gabriella Keen's world tilted on its axis.

***

Ash remained impassive for all of a moment while the little minx pressed her mouth firmly to his. Then he moved fast as lightning, taking control of their first kiss.

The feel of her warm, lush body pressed willingly against him was almost too much for him to take. Ash knew he should push her away. He knew this was not right. He did not deserve a mate. For a few minutes there, he'd allowed himself the pleasure of looking after her, taking care of her, when Aphrodite handed the little inebriated female over to him.

"You do anything out of bounds, Asmodeus, and I will wreak my revenge on you tenfold. But since I am pretty sure she is your mate, here. Now, you take care of her. Her name is Gabriella Keen, and I believe her Wolf is going to be making an appearance soon. It is her first Change. She will need your help," the Goddess instructed.

Oh fuck.

Oh Fuck.

OH FUCK.

Trying to defy his natural response to her was like trying to stop a tsunami with an umbrella or dampen an inferno with a thimbleful of water. Impossible.

And why should he even bother when it felt so damn good?

Because you are damned, Ash.

You almost destroyed the world once.

How could you possibly deserve her?

But even that did not stop him from wanting to explore every inch of her plush frame with his lips and hands and teeth. Ash wanted to explore the depths of passion between her plump thighs with his tongue, to taste and swallow her juices, until she cried out in pleasure and scored his back with her fingernails. He wanted to sink into her heat, to thrust into her core, and bring them both to an ecstatic, soul searing bliss that he'd been searching for his whole life. The Demon of Lust wanted her. Period. And that was why he had to give her up.

Grrr.

His Demonic side did not like that idea. Not one bit. In fact, he felt his claws protrude from his fingernails as her hot tongue boldly invaded his mouth. Holy hell, the little schoolteacher could kiss. Her delightfully headfirst reaction was his undoing. She sucked on his tongue, causing that other part of him to ache and throb with need. She raked her teeth across his lower lip, moaning into his mouth as she pressed her plush breasts even tighter against his chest.

On and on the kiss went until Ash hardly recalled moving with her until they both lay on the sofa. He smoothed the skirt of the little black dress she wore until it was up around her waist.

Her searching hands roamed his

back, until she cupped his ass, and, fuck, he really almost lost it. Gabriella parted her legs, cushioning him between her thighs. She rolled her hips, flexing her molten core against his still covered cock, and his eyes rolled back.

"Ash," she moaned his name, tilting her head to allow him access to her throat.

Fucking hell.

He was a goner.

Ash licked the long column of her neck, nibbling at her clavicle. Her skin tasted divine. That same raspberry lime scent covering her skin exploded on his tongue.

He wanted more.

He wanted it all.

"Oh yes," she whispered, her hands

in his hair as he found the zipper to her dress, parting it so he could pull it down, exposing her incredible bosoms.

The hardened nubs were like ripe berries, like fruit so pure and sweet, they should be forbidden to the likes of him. But Ash had not the will power to deny himself. He lowered his head, sucking one into his mouth, teasing and twirling the nubbin with his tongue.

Arousal sizzled like an electrical current between them. So hot and strong, his whole body was burning with it. He was out of control, and so was she. He knew it. Knew then he could never take her like this. Mindless with desire and beyond her own experience.

No.

When he did finally have her, it was

going to be with her eyes wide open. His heart squeezed, beating thunderously inside of him. Ash wanted nothing more than to bury himself deep within her, but she was no quick fuck. No trifle to bang and toss aside.

Mine.

That voice inside him growled the word more forcefully this time. Followed by another even more potent word.

Mate.

Resigned to a night of suffering blue balls and cold showers, Ash slowed his kisses. Gabby moaned, lifting her glassy, lust-glazed eyes to his. He read the hurt and confusion, the lust still there.

"We have to stop now," he told her.

"Oh, oh god! I am so sorry," she said, pushing him off, and he eased back, refusing to allow her to continue the train of thought he could read so easily in her eyes.

"No. Listen to me. I want you. Desperately. I know you can feel that I do," he murmured, smiling when she blushed.

"Then why are you stopping?" Gabby asked.

"Because when we do this, and we *will* do this, Gabriella. But when that time comes, I want you to be fully aware of the consequences," Ash stated. "I will not play games. Not with you, Gabriella. You've just discovered this world, this other part to who you are. Let me help you navigate it. Then you can decide what it is you want."

"Really? You would do that for me?"

she asked, bewilderment easily displayed in her gaze.

"I would do anything for you."

And surprisingly enough, he meant it. He sat up then, helping her to rearrange her dress. When she would've done it herself, he stilled her hands, placing a small kiss on her lips while he slid the zipper up, covering her beauty from his eyes. It was the most difficult thing he'd ever had to do. A true test of his honor, he supposed. When all he really wanted was to tear the hateful clothing off her skin and keep her in his bed where he could pleasure her nonstop for a month or two.

"That sounds interesting," she said, grinning, and he realized he'd spoken out loud.

"You know, I've got the distinct feeling you've rendered me unguarded. I am vulnerable with you, Gabriella."

"Is that bad?"

"It is when you are the General of the Daemonium Guard," he muttered.

"Is that what you do? You're some kind of warrior?"

"Yes," he nodded. "We protect the Underworld from invasion. Patrolling the borders and keeping the soulless ones, rogues who lost themselves to the darkness, at bay is our prime directive."

"Oh, wow. I'm just a teacher, and not even a real one right now."

"What do you mean?"

"Oh, well, I'm sort of in between jobs. Right now, I am teaching catechism classes."

"I see," he replied, amused at her sudden bashfulness.

"I guess I should go home. I have class tomorrow afternoon."

"Okay," he said, his voice growing hoarse.

"I'll take you."

Ash stood up, his whole body trembling with emotion.

Was it creepy if he hid himself from sight and stayed within a reasonable distance?

Like in her backyard?

Fuck.

Yes, that was creepy. Even for him. But his chest positively ached when he thought of leaving her home.

"Ash?" her quiet voice reached him, and he spun round on his heels to look at her sweet face.

"Yes?"

"Would it be okay, that is, I don't want to sound like a nut, but could I stay here tonight? I just feel better, here, with you," she said the last two words so lowly he wasn't quite sure he'd heard her correctly.

"You want to stay here?"

"I can sleep on the couch—"

"No!" he said forcefully.

"You're right. Good grief, I can't believe I even suggested that. I am sorry if I overstepped—"

"No, that's not what I meant. I meant yes, *yes,* Gabby. Of course, you can stay here, but *no* it will not be on my couch. Come, you shall have my room."

She would sleep in comfort, and he

would stand guard over her. Even if it killed him to have her so close and not touch her.

A test of willpower maybe?

Allowing her this close tonight, only to take her back to the surface tomorrow, might just kill him. But he would not die. No way. He had so much to look forward to with her in his life. This was simply a test. A really fucking tough test of his willpower and desire to put her needs first. His body strained, hands itching to touch, lips wanting to kiss, and cock twitching, eager to plunder.

Fucking hell.

Asmodeus, Demon of Lust, was in for one extremely uncomfortable night. Oh well. His dick would survive, he mused.

He was a soldier, after all. And better suffer with her in his home than have her leave it.

Yeah. His body would be fine being near her and keeping his hands to himself, no matter how difficult. He just didn't know if his heart would be.

Grrr.

CHAPTER EIGHT

GABRIELLA STRETCHED AND met the dawn, or what passed for it in the Underworld, with a small yawn and tired eyes, blinking against the reddish orange glow streaming in from the drapes.

It was a little strange, but she was fine. In fact, she'd never slept so peacefully in her life. The silk sheets felt so good beneath her, even if they were black. A color that reminded her of sex and sin, though she'd never really indulged all that much.

They made her feel decadent and naughty.

Imagine a Sunday school teacher on black silk!

She knew full well she'd done nothing even remotely sinful, but still, it was fun to pretend. At least, she was not alone in her desires. Ash had wanted her too. It was sort of noble the way he'd stopped before things got out of control. She appreciated that and was frustrated by it at the same time.

The coverlet on top of her was the same inky dark shade as the sheets. The lightweight blanket was perfect considering how warm the air was in Purgatory. She still could not believe it, but Ash had told her all about the place where he dwelled.

The Underworld was real. As were Shifters, Witches, Demons, Angels, and a myriad of other creatures. Imps too, of course.

His home was gorgeous, even though he'd called it small. Obviously, the Demon had never rented an apartment on the Lower East Side in Manhattan. This place was positively enormous by comparison.

Besides the enormous, comfortable bed, and luxurious coverings was the best bonus of all. That came in the shape of a snuggly, muscled pillow beneath her head. Gabriella could have stayed there forever. She'd felt so safe and cherished with him.

Foolish?

Maybe.

But she did not think so. She even fell asleep in Ash's embrace. Not the least bit uncomfortable with him, which was shocking considering she'd known him all of a minute.

He was surprisingly warm to the touch. As she stirred, his arms came around her gently and he rubbed her back and nuzzled the top of her head.

So nice and cozy!

She smiled against his pale, smooth skin.

Gabriella felt chilled most of the time, always had. But being near Ash, snuggling up to him in his enormous bed, was the warmest she'd ever felt. Even if the Demon in question spent the night on the bed, on top of the blanket instead of beneath it with her. She'd refused to take his bed entirely.

"Morning," he murmured, and she sighed.

"Good morning."

His heart beat steadily beneath her ear and Gabriella was ridiculously happy just lying there with him, listening to the strong *thump-thump thump-thump* rhythm. Her mind raced with everything that happened the previous night.

Girl meets Mim for dinner. Mim spills crazy beans about Wolf inside of the girl. Mim introduces more supernatural surprises. Girl meets Goddess and Vampire. Goddess and Vampire set girl

ASH

up with speed dating thingy in Underworld bar. Girl gets drunk. Girl meets Demon. Girl jumps Demon and steals bed.

This was it. The moment she'd been aiming for since high school. Gabby was a total slut. Or a slut wannabe. She didn't actually do much that would earn her that title. And all because her *cutie patootie*, Ash, did not want to take advantage of her.

Ever since she'd been voted *Miss Goody Two Shoes* of her graduating class in high school, Gabriella had attempted to shed her image. But it never worked out for her. Last night had crossed several firsts off her list.

She'd gotten drunk, made out with a virtual stranger, but stopped short of sleeping with him. Leave it to Gabby to find the one honorable Demon in the Underworld!

The irony was not lost on her.

What did a gal have to do to get a little lovin', anyway?

Her body swelled and ached, and she felt him tense beneath her. Gabby breathed in a great, deep breath, loving the masculine scent wafting off him. Like sandalwood and something else, something dark and spicy that made her belly heat and her panties damp.

Mine.

Lick.

Nibble.

The words appeared in her mind, but she knew they were not from her. Not exactly, anyway. She felt her muscles tense and her belly quiver. She felt something pushing, scratching against her skin. Not unpleasant exactly, but strange, foreign.

Oooh.

Something was off.

Not off.

Mine.

Ours.

Mate.

Bite.

"Hey, you alright?" Ash's concerned voice brought her eyes flashing up to his dark ones.

She'd never seen eyes like that. Not brown or gray, more like slate. Yes! That was it! His eyes glittered like slate, then they turned completely black. She wondered if that was always true when his emotions were heightened.

Did he see in black and white when they got like that?

Questions, so many questions raced through her mind, and feelings. But fear was not one of them. Never that.

"Red," he said.

"What?"

"When I am very emotional, I see red," he explained.

"You know, I have the distinct impression we are reading each other's minds sometimes," she whispered."

"Perhaps. It happens when mates bond."

"Mates? You started saying something yesterday," she began, but he was already kissing her and ending the kiss far too soon.

Once more, she growled deep in her chest. This time she welcomed the rush of power that came with it, refusing to give in to the dizzying wave of lightheadedness and the twinge of pain. Darn it. She hated not feeling well.

"What is that? Why does that keep happening?" she asked and stood up.

"That is your Wolf, my sweet. She is gaining presence. Soon you will experience your first Change. It will hurt, Gabriella," he told her, frowning as he spoke.

"Hurt?"

"Yes, and I am sorry that I cannot help with that."

Gabby's eyes bulged out of her head.

How the heck was she supposed to do that in one of the most crowded cities in the world?

Would someone see her?

Was she dangerous?

Would it hurt very badly?

For the first time since meeting him, panic threatened to overwhelm her. But it left just as quickly as it came when he placed both hands on her shoulders, encouraging her gaze to meet his.

"You will be safe, Gabriella. I swear it."

She looked down, turning into him for comfort. Her vision was suddenly blurry with tears. His words soothed her. Yes, he was, for all intents and purposes, a stranger, but she felt closer to him than anyone else in the world.

Gabriella was drawn to him in ways she could not express with words. She felt she could trust him. And yes, silly as it might be, she believed his words. Ash would protect her. She knew it deep inside her heart.

Mine.

"What time is it?" she asked, trying for a calm she did not feel.

"Time is irrelevant here, but on Earth it is noon," he replied.

"Oh my, I have to go!"

"Alright, I will take you to the portal once I have fed you."

"No, I'm not hungr—"

Gabriella stopped, face flaming as her stomach rumbled. Yes, she was hungry. Yes, it was the typical chubby girl move. But oh well. She liked food. It was a fact she could hardly deny.

"Ernie would have prepared a feast

for us by now," he grinned, taking her hand, and stopping at the large bathroom.

He motioned for her to use the facilities first, and Gabby's heart swelled at his thoughtfulness. No one had ever treated her with such respect and tenderness before. She could really get used to that.

"And you shall," he whispered, kissing her hand and ushering her inside the bathroom. He closed the door reluctantly, and she leaned against it, expelling a sigh.

The bathroom was impressive in its size and tasteful extravagance. Black glass tiles and countertops with a glass door enclosed six-headed shower on one side, and a huge sunken tub on another.

She really hoped she got the chance to use both.

With him.

Oh yes.

Her increasingly familiar inner voice whispered once more in her head, and she grinned. Gabriella was beginning to recognize it as part of her. Her Wolf perhaps. Anyway, she had a feeling that would come in handy.

She brushed her teeth with the spare toothbrush that appeared on the counter, used the toilet, washed her hands and face, and brushed her hair, braiding it into a neat bun at her nape. There was nothing to be done about the wrinkled state of her dress, but she felt presentable, at least. Her complexion was clear and her blue eyes bright, despite her overindulgence the night before.

"You look beautiful," Ash said the moment she rejoined him.

"Don't you have to use the bathroom?" she asked.

"I used the guest one while you were in there," he said, and held out a chair for her in the dining room.

A number of dishes covered the table. Everything smelled wonderful. There was an entire glazed ham, small roasted potatoes, Danishes, bagels, croissants, fresh fruits and cheeses, smoked lox, poached eggs, and a mountain of waffles.

"How many people are you feeding?" She gasped, astounded at the sheer amount of food.

"How do you mean?"

"Never mind," she said, turning when she heard the clicking of Ernie's clawed legs on the marble floors.

"Good morning, Ernie. I'm Gabby."

The Imp looked from Gabby to Ash, and back to Gabby once more. He swallowed nervously, ducking his head as if embarrassed. A day ago she would have been creeped out by this strange creature, but she felt her heart warming to him. Ernie was actually quite sweet.

"Morning, mistress."

"This is Gabriella, Ernie. You may call her by her name," Ash said kindly.

"Yes, Mast—, I mean, yes, Boss," he corrected himself.

"You see, the entire Underworld has gone through a complete change at

Lucifer's whim. I have only just returned after being away for some time, but Ernie here has been in my employ for centuries. It will take time to adjust, but we will get through it. Won't we, Ernie?"

"Yes, M—, I mean, Boss," he replied, placing a fresh urn of coffee on the table.

"The coffee smells wonderful, Ernie, thank you," Gabby said to Ernie.

"Oh, the missus is to take credit for that. She roasted the beans with magic and brewed them herself!" Ernie smiled, showing three short, sharp teeth in his mouth. His face was so full of joy at her praise!

Gabby grinned and asked him to thank his wife for her, and he promised he would. Fascinating, she thought.

Ernie left to finish other duties, and

ASH

Gabby was surprisingly comfortable alone with Ash. They ate in companionable silence with the odd question here and there. She was uncertain what would happen next. Her time with him was ending, but he said he would help her through her Change. She wondered if he meant that.

"The portal back to Earth is just this way," Ash said, frowning.

"What's wrong?"

"Nothing." Ash shrugged.

"Something is bothering you."

"Well, it's just I hate to leave you, but I must check on the legions I oversee."

"We both have work, Ash, that's alright. Will I see you later, though?" Gabby asked tentatively. She did not want to seem needy, but this was a first for her. That inner voice of hers growled at the thought of leaving him, but she had things to tend to. So did he.

Would he think her desperate now?

Oh well.

Gabriella was a lot of things, but patient was not one of them. She did not play games. Her tendency toward bluntness was sometimes off putting to men, but she couldn't help it. If she liked someone, she told them. And the truth could be said if she did not like someone as well.

"Of course," he replied to her earlier question. "Gabriella, this is just the beginning. Once you've had your first Change, you will understand what I mean."

"I don't know why you just won't tell

me already," she mumbled, and he laughed. The rat.

"Ah, here we are. Gabriella, allow me to introduce you to the Sphinx."

Gabriella stuttered in her steps. There, before her, stood a massive stone and metal gateway. But that was not what had her tongue-tied. It was the equally enormous half-Lion, half-woman guarding the portal with a grin on her face that made her want to run away or point and gasp.

"Asmodeus, I welcome you to the portal. A riddle first—"

"Seriously? Do you not recognize me? I am Asmodeus. Also known as Ashmedai. I am a Prince of Hell. General of the Daemonium Guard. You, Sphinx, can save your riddles for someone lesser," Ash hissed, flexing his wings which had suddenly made a magnificent appearance.

Gabriella's mouth dropped open. Holy cow. It seemed her speed dating partner was something of a big shot down in the Underworld.

A general?

Was that some kind of military thing then?

Hmmm. She'd think on that later. Right then, Gabriella was preoccupied with the imposing figure he made with his wings, horns and tail filling her vision.

How imposing!

How totally hot!

And also, totally unnecessary.

Gabriella could handle herself against

a riddle or two. She was a teacher, for Pete's sake. She knew a lot of things.

"I am the Keeper of the Gate, Ash, and you can't tell me who to challenge. I answer to Lucifer alone—"

"And who do you think I answer to? Tell me, will the Lord of the Underworld be pleased with your idiotic display?" Ash seethed, but Gabriella had seen enough. She was not about to allow this to escalate. Even if seeing him like that turned her on.

OMG!

She really was a freak.

Sigh.

"Ash," she said, placing her hand on his elbow. "It's fine, really. What's your riddle?"

CHAPTER NINE

ASH WANTED TO rage at the she-beast.
There was really no other way to
describe his intense anger at the
Sphinx's stupid hoity toity fucking face.
How dare she stop him and toss one of
her puzzles at his mate! Such arrogance
was not to be tolerated, and she should
damn well know it.

ASH

"Thank you, my lady," the half-Lion bitch said, and Ash snarled angrily.

"I got this," Gabriella said, leaning her back against his chest.

He tucked her in closer, wrapping his arms around her waist as if he'd been doing that all his life. Seemed natural. Like he was supposed to hold her like that. Anyway, he fucking liked it, so he wasn't going to stop. Unless she told him to.

"A special one for you, lady fair," the Sphinx sneered, and Ash made a mental note to inform Lucifer of her highhandedness with his mate.

As mate to the General of the Daemonium Guard, Ash expected Gabriella to not have to participate in these petty games. Her clearance should be on par with his. He would see it done. Later.

"With pointed fangs, I sit and wait," she began with a smirk on her face. "With piercing force, I crunch out fate. Grabbing victims, proclaiming might, physically joining with a single bite. What am I, mistress? Tell me, and you may pass," the Sphinx grinned with a curtsy.

"I suppose because I am a newcomer to the Underworld, you expect me to answer with something like a Demon, Imp, or Vampire, don't you?" Gabriella asked, her blue eyes glittering with mischief.

"Is that your answer?"

Ash tensed. He hated riddles, and while he was old enough to know better, he tended to jump at the wrong answer or simply end whatever game had begun with good, old-fashioned fisticuffs.

Grrr.

"No, Sphinx. It's not. My answer is this," Gabriella said, crooking her finger and beckoning the Sphinx closer.

Ash frowned, lip curled as the Sphinx lowered her body to the ground. He could tell the arrogant cat beast expected her to guess wrong, but Ash had faith.

"The answer to your riddle, what sits and waits with pointed fangs crunching out fate and joining with a bite, is simple. It's a stapler."

"Wro— Hey! You guessed it!"

"Of course, I did. I'm a teacher," Gabriella said with a satisfied grin on her face.

Ash growled, enjoying watching the Sphinx hastily rise and open the portal. He hissed as he passed, making certain the half-Lion woman was aware of his displeasure.

"My lord," she murmured, trying to show respect, but it was too late to appease him.

"Next time, no riddles," Ash growled.

"No, General, of course," Sphinx said, averting her gaze.

"Come on, Ash. I don't want to be late."

He'd worried she might be angry with his handling of the Sphinx, but Gabriella seemed unaffected. Another facet of the magnificent female. He grinned and took her hand, tucking her close while the portal zipped them up to the Earth's surface.

The arid heat of LA greeted them on the other side, but Ash was unaffected as he maneuvered them to the place where she'd left her car the night before. Climbing in the passenger seat, he watched Gabriella don her seatbelt and check her mirrors before heading out into the late morning traffic.

"What time is your class?"

"Oh, it's not 'till this evening. But I have to get changed and prepare my notes."

"I see," he listened, realizing he had his own work to do.

Tension rain through him as he walked her to the door. He could not help but stare, his longing gaze roaming over her from head to toe. He did not want to go, but even as he stood trying to figure out how to say farewell, he felt someone calling him from below.

"What time will you be finished?"

"Catechism class starts at five and ends around seven," she replied, her blue eyes wide and staring up at him like twin sapphire pools.

"Where?"

"Um, over at St. Rose's," she replied, licking her lips, unconsciously drawing his attention to her soft pink rosebud of a mouth.

"I will be there waiting."

Yes, it was bold of him to assume she wanted to see him again. Even bolder to simply state he would be there to pick her up, but she did not seem to mind.

His beautiful Gabriella nodded, eyes flashing blue fire as he leaned in to crush his mouth against hers.

Kissing her was easily the best thing he'd ever experienced in his very long lifetime. She molded to him, wrapping her arms lovingly around his neck as she gave and gave and asked nothing in return. But he returned it tenfold or more. All his passion and experience, all his desire and need, every drop of what he felt for the new Wolf was there in that kiss.

"Gabby!" Someone shouted from inside, and a snarl tore out of his throat as he hastily moved her behind him.

Gabby chuckled into his back and her arms wrapped around his waist from behind as she stilled his instinctive move to attack whoever was screeching that way. How dare someone interrupt them!

"It's okay," his sweet told him. "That's just Mim."

"Gabriella Keen! You never come home at— Oh! Hello, there!" A tall, thin blonde who smelled of Wolf and citrus entered the foyer.

Ash did not return her greeting, merely cocked his head to the side as he used his Demonic powers to read her aura. No evil there. None that he could see. That meant this Mim was the good person Gabriella believed her to be. With that knowledge in hand, Ash nodded his greeting.

"Hello, I am Ash."

"Well, thank you for bringing her home, Ash. Will you two be seeing each other again?"

"Mim!" Gabby hissed.

"Of course," Ash replied, unfazed by his soon-to-be-mate's response.

"I see," Mim said, eyes flashing gold with her she-Wolf. "Gabby, please come into the kitchen when you are finished here. Nice to meet you, Ash. Looking forward to it again," she replied and went back inside the large house.

"I am so sorry about that!" Gabby said, moving in front of him.

He liked that her arms remained around his waist. Liked that she touched him without invitation or fear. All these sensations were new and honest, as were her actions. And they felt so damn good, he knew he could never give them up. Or her.

"Why should you apologize? She loves and protects you, that is a good thing, Gabriella."

"I know, but, well, I am so embarrassed," she murmured, covering her eyes briefly. "I don't do this often. Stay out all night, and come home with strange men—"

"Good. Then I won't have to hunt anyone down and kill them," he replied without thinking, but she just giggled and hugged him tighter.

Nice that she approved. Though, he had a feeling she might've thought him kidding. Oh well. They could clear that up later.

Ash growled as someone called him again from the Underworld. One of his legates, he was sure, though he could not discern which one. Fucker was trying to summon him, and Ash was going to carve a nice chunk of his hide from his body when he appeared. No one summoned the General, save Lucifer himself.

"I will see you at St. Rose's, then, around seven?" Ash whispered, tracing the lines of her face before kissing her lips softly. Anything more and he could not tear himself away.

"Are you sure you want to see me again?"

"Foolish woman, of course I do. Besides, I promised to help you with your Wolf. It is the full moon tonight. I imagine she will want out."

"I almost forgot about that," she said, looking down.

"Gabriella, that isn't the only reason I will be back."

"It's not?"

"No," he said, tracing her lower lip with his thumb.

She was so beautiful it almost hurt to look at her. His heart squeezed painfully at the strength of his feelings for her, but he didn't care. He reveled in it. Looked forward to learning how much more he would feel when he made her his.

"Alright. Later, then," she said, and he could tell she was having a hard time walking away too.

Ash kissed her again, eyes open so he could watch the sweet expression on her face. Fuck, he already cared too much. He forced himself to gently set her away from him.

ASH

Demons were born of fire and brimstone, but they were nothing if not passionate. Of course, passion could take on many forms. He'd never expected love to be one of them, and yet, that was the only word that came to mind when he held this precious woman in his arms.

"Yes," he replied. "I will see you later, Gabriella."

She waved goodbye before closing the door, her blue eyes watching him through the thick glass panes. He nodded his head, urging her to retreat lest he stand there all day, and finally, she turned away with a small smile and a faint blush staining her cheeks. He waited until he could no longer see her before turning to answer the incessant call of one of his legates.

Ironically, there was a portal far closer to Gabriella's home than he'd previously known. Within ten minutes, he was back in the Underworld, and in rare form. The Daemonium Guard was one of the most elite units in the Underworld. Some would argue they were the best of the best.

He entered their command center, his black eyes zeroing in on the one who dared summon him. The fucker was looking back at him, as if he had not earned the respect he demanded from his lessors.

Ash snarled, his horns, tail, and wings in full effect. He felt his magic call to the fire of the pit and felt it circling him, causing those in the room to give him a wide berth. Okay, so he was cranky. BFD. These fuckers had to be hard and ready for anything in their line of work.

They were no good to the Underworld if they scurried like cockroaches at their leaders' wrath. He would dismiss them readily if they did. He needed his legions tough, brutal, and fierce. Theirs was not a task for the soft and ill prepared. Ash's ruthlessness for stupidity and laziness was renowned.

Those in attendance stopped what they were doing the second he'd appeared. Standing at attention, they froze in place, each of them perfect warriors with skills honed to defend, protect, and keep the Underworld from those things evil and other that would dare try to seize what Lucifer had claimed for himself.

Being appointed General of the Daemonium Guard was an honor and a very grave duty. Ash took his responsibilities seriously. He only employed the best, most fearsome Demons and residents of Purgatory for the job. Which was why he was so fucking pissed at them. With a mighty snarl, he entered the room.

"What is so terrible that my hand chosen legates cannot contain it without calling me like an injured babe calling for his mother?"

"My liege," the legate in question, a Demon named Heinrich, finally looked down, averting his gaze in that same respectful manner that was his due.

ASH

"Apologies, my liege, but I thought you needed to see this," he mumbled, holding out his tablet.

It seemed everyone was online these days. Even in the Underworld. Just another modern annoyance, in his opinion. Okay, fine, so he enjoyed the ability to monitor his legions from his office without relying on some seer to report to him.

Ash growled deep and low, still annoyed at the Demon's gall in summoning him. Only the sound of someone chuckling from inside his own office stopped him in his tracks.

It seemed Lucifer himself was in residence. Fabulous. Like Ash needed more interruptions. He glanced down at the proffered tablet and frowned. Fuck.

This was serious. A large number of the soulless were gathering at the same southern border he was worried about earlier.

"Send legions eight and fifteen on the double. And make sure Vanth is updated. The number of soulless has tripled in the past forty-eight hours with no one's notice! Unacceptable! I want reports, now. I want to know who missed this, and I want the legate in front of me on the double!" he roared.

"Yes, my liege," grunted the Demon as Ash handed him back his tablet.

Without sparing another glance at the men in the room, he headed for his office door. Inside was Lucifer, larger than life, sitting at his desk, with his feet on the otherwise polished surface.

Fucker.

"Ah! There you are! Well?"

"Well, what?" Ash asked as his wings, horns, and tail receded.

"How was speed dating?"

"How did you even know I went?" He tried changing the subject, but the Lord of the Underworld was not stupid.

"Would my most loyal Demon disobey an order? Come on, spill!" Lucifer's grin was wicked as he slammed a fist on the table.

Seemed he was not going anywhere without news, so Ash sat down and crossed his legs. He brushed some lint from his coat, knowing that Lucifer was damn near to blowing a gasket.

"I met someone," Ash announced before his boss could erupt like a bloody volcano in his workspace.

"So, you admit, I was right? Ha! Tell me, old man. Who is she? Where is she? Does she live here or up top?"

He exhaled, rolling his shoulders, and trying to put a damper on the excitement he felt. He did not want to appear overeager, but there was no denying he cared for her. So, he told Lucifer about Gabriella, noting the man's excitement that he too was fated to a Werewolf.

"This is fantastic, Ashmedai! I could not be more pleased. Have you told her yet? About being your fated mate and living here with you—"

"Not yet, no," he said, interrupting Lucifer at his own peril. "But I will."

He had to. Ash had a long way to go before he felt worthy of the sweet female, but he knew one thing for certain.

Gabriella Keen was his.

"My liege?"

Ash turned with a scowl at the sound of the interruption.

"Forgive me, but they need you on the southern border. The soulless are starting to overrun our legions!"

"Fucking hell," he snarled.

"Better see to that," Lucifer commanded, but Ash was already off.

Shit.

He'd much rather be on his way to pick up Gabriella, but it was Ash's duty to be battle ready, if not eager for a fight. Besides, knowing she would be his one day was an incentive to rid the Underworld of the nefarious creatures threatening its stability. Above all other things, her safety was of the utmost importance.

"Legates! At the ready!" Ash shouted.

He bowed to Lucifer and exited the office, exhaling slowly at the responding growls and snarling from his elite warriors. Swords, maces, semiautomatics, and a variety of weapons in hand, his men saluted, falling in line behind him as he led them outdoors at a brisk pace.

The Daemonium Guard had their own secret portals to traverse the Underworld. It was the only way to do what they did in any reasonable amount of time. Chest heaving, he psyched himself up to investigate and, if necessary, put an end to the soulless' invasion. He faced his men before entering the tunnel that would bring them to the southern border in seconds and repeated the Daemonium creed.

"*Sanguine et sudore nostra defendimus!*"

The words were old but potent. Translated, it meant *with blood and sweat we defend what is ours*. What else would a Guard do, after all? But it was the response that made all who'd heard of them fear the Daemonium Guard, those that protected the Underworld's borders, led by the ruthless General Asmodeus.

"*Ut dolor!*" The legates snarled their response in unison.

To the pain, Ash translated snarling wickedly. And that was a promise. They would defend their lands to the pain of anyone who dared test them. There were things worse than death. Much worse. Ash could attest to that himself. It felt good to be on the giving end, rather than the receiving.

True, he had a lot to overcome in order to feel worthy of his sweet, but if love ever was a motivator, then now was the time. Ash flexed his wings, glad that he'd worn jeans and a simple shirt to escort Gabby back home. He had no time to change if he wanted to be on time. And he would be on time to pick her up without fail. Always.

Pushing his mate's sweetness from his mind was difficult, but he managed it. All he had to do to accomplish that was focus on her well being. No one would threaten his future mate's safety and live to tell the tale.

Snarrrlll.

CHAPTER TEN

WAS IT WRONG for her stomach to do flip flops just thinking about Ash?

She sighed as she handed out glue sticks and bits of this and that for her CCD class to use on their art project. The kids had behaved so nicely for her after story time, and now, they were happy and excited over their art projects.

ASH

Gabby wondered if it was wrong of her to be there. After all, she'd spent the night in Purgatory. Guilt was not something she felt comfortable with, so she went to ask Fr. Perez.

"Father? I have a question—"

But the friendly, round-faced priest of her childhood put down his cell phone and turned to face her with sadness in his eyes. One hand was behind his back, as if he was hiding something, and he appeared almost like a stranger to her. Something inside of her growled, her other half pressing against her skin in a way that had her stumbling ungracefully. There was a bitter smell in the air that made it hard to breathe.

"I cannot help you anymore, child," the stoutly priest said, making the sign of the cross with his free hand. "God forgive me," he whispered so silently, she would not have heard if not for her supernaturally enhanced hearing capabilities.

So cool.

Gabby paused, unable to revel in her new superpowers since something was decidedly off with the priest. She took a sniff. That new part of her that was waking up, her *she-Wolf,* growled a warning. Without being conscious of it, Gabby swung out with her arm, blocking the massive blade Fr. Perez had drawn on her.

He'd been aiming the pointy side straight at her heart.

What the heck?

Her childhood priest sneered,

struggling to free the deadly sword from where it was now stuck in the marble of the statue.

Thank goodness for her quick reflexes!

But why was Fr. Perez wielding a sword?

Was he suddenly into a little *D&D* roleplaying or something?

Realization dawned and her chest squeezed painfully. The priest she had known most of her life was brandishing a medieval weapon against her.

To hurt her.

Maybe even kill her.

Holy cow!

What the what was going on?

Anger coursed through her, and she struggled with it for a moment before narrowing her eyes at the man who was once so familiar and was now a total stranger. Gabby straightened her back and used her best teacher's voice on the pale and pudgy priest.

"Fr. Perez! What *are* you doing?"

He froze on the spot. Clearly shocked by her tone, which was something she'd worked very hard on as a teacher to gently discipline unruly children, especially the preschoolers. Gabby usually offered some form of praise to reward her students after they'd been scolded, but she wasn't feeling all that kind toward Fr. Perez at the moment.

Especially since he was still intent on attacking her with the enormous blade.

Grrr.

Yay for Werewolf super strength.

"I've known you all my life!" she exclaimed, using very little force to hold the blade at bay.

"You are not the woman I know, Gabby! I could ignore your Werewolf side so long as it was dormant, but now that it has awoken, I must take action! I have to prove my loyalty to mankind!" The chubby priest grunted and tried to free his sword from where she still had it pinned against a marble statue of St. Rose, to no avail.

"First, I think you mean *humankind*, and second, how do you know about any of this?" Gabby asked, correcting him first on his chauvinism.

"The Council knows all! Now, release my blade and I will dispel of you quickly," he grunted. "In the name of the

Father..." Fr. Perez prayed aloud, using his foot against the pedestal of the statue to try and gain leverage.

Dang it.

Gabby really liked that statue. It was part of the history and artistry of the Catholic Church that she loved to study so much. So much blood and violence, she supposed she should not be surprised at a priest wielding a sword. The Church certainly had a messy past, and one of Gabby's fondest interests in college had been her church history classes.

It was not surprising they hid their connection to the supernatural world.

Who would believe it in this day and age, anyway?

Still, how could he be so small

minded?

Gabby frowned at Fr. Perez and his incessant struggles.

"Enough of this," she growled, then tugged on the blade, sending the whimpering priest to his knees.

He muttered a prayer, held up his crucifix, and shouted at her with spittle flying from his lips.

Okay, that was just gross. And now she was annoyed. Life might have taken one hell of a turn just recently, but that didn't mean everyone had to lose their manners, for Pete's sake!

"You will not prevail," Fr. Perez yelled, still drooling.

How uncouth!

"Heed me, doer of evil! I do not fear you! If you must end my life in the name of our Lord—"

"What are you talking about? You're the one with the sword! I was only teaching my class. For heaven's sake, get up," she growled, and hoisted him by the arm.

The ease with which she lifted the portly man was surprising and elating. But Gabby had no time to enjoy her newfound strength. She was hurt and upset.

She had reason to be.

The man tried to kill her!

"Who were you on the phone with before I walked in here?" Gabby asked, angrily mashing her teeth together, so she didn't do something really bad, like curse out the idiotic man inside the church.

"He is known only as the Spaniard. A blessed God-fearing Christian! Unlike you, *hell spawn*. He is in charge of the Council, for now, giving orders via Rome herself! The Hounds of God are no more. There is no keeping *your kind* in line! That means we good Catholics must act—"

"Quiet! You know something, I have had enough of this. Fr. Perez, I am shocked and appalled by your behavior," she said, waving the sword. "I have been part of your congregation for most of my life. You gave me the sacraments of Communion and Confirmation yourself! So, what are you saying? That I am evil just because I am a Werewolf?"

"Exactly! Then you understand why you must die!"

"You are crazy, and I don't think any God would condone murder regardless of creed. Shame on you!" Gabby growled.

She was completely scandalized. She'd heard of people being grossly prejudicial against others for just about every reason imaginable, but she'd never been on the tail end of it. Never imagined in all of her life that someone would want to kill her simply because of what she was. Gabby didn't choose to be a Werewolf.

And even if she did, so what?

Why hate her?

Why try to kill her?

This seriously blows!

Her thoughts surprised even her. She tried hard not to squeak at her own use of language. She never cursed, but boy, was she close!

"No!" Fr. Perez said, nodding his head. "You are the evil one, Gabby. Werewolves cannot be good. That is it in a nutshell, I am afraid. And I am sorry it must be this way. I hoped I was wrong, but Gabby, it seems your stepmother has corrupted you. Yes, my former child, you are my enemy now."

"But you hired me to teach catechism class?"

"Ah yes, well, you are fired!" Fr. Perez exclaimed, waving his finger angrily.

What?

Oh, that was just great!

She did not know what was worse. That she was being fired from her job, or that Fr. Perez, her childhood priest, was trying to kill her because of some priest-

Werewolf prejudice. Both were unconscionable. And to be honest, it sorta hurt.

"You know something, Father? I was raised Catholic, and I take that to heart. I hold many of the traditions of our faith sacred, and just because I am a Werewolf does not mean I can't be a good Catholic. Now, I don't need to be in this building to pray to God, so I will leave. But shame on you! Shame on everyone who thinks like you," she said angrily, reining in the desire to rip his throat out.

Oooh, that's a new one.

Gabby was never prone to violence, but she sure felt like it just then.

"And you know what?" she asked the priest, waving the heavy sword around as easily as a toothpick. "I am taking this with me!"

Gabby grabbed the heavy blade and went to the back room to gather her belongings. The two mothers who volunteered as aids for the Catechism classes looked at her questioningly when she walked past them with the sword, but she just shook her head. They would figure it out, eventually.

Sighing in annoyance, Gabby hefted her laptop bag, pocketbook, supply bag, and sword, and walked to her car. How inconsiderate of Fr. Perez to fire her after she'd already bought a new planner! Gabby mumbled under her breath as she pressed the button on her key fob to pop her trunk, placing the bags and sword inside.

Ugh.

She checked her phone and sighed. Twenty minutes to kill until Ash showed up. No way she was leaving him there to be greeted by whatever else Fr. Perez had hidden up his robe.

Eww.

She shook her head when her mind went right to the gutter. First time for everything, she supposed. Her stomach cramped uncomfortably, and Gabby closed her eyes. It was too soon for her period, but the pains she was experiencing bore a striking resemblance to her cycle.

Ouch!

The heat seemed to close in on her, despite the fact her skin was chilled. Gabby gasped, trying to catch her breath. Her head felt foggy, and her stomach clenched. Mim had explained earlier she'd never been very sick as a child because of her Werewolf genes, but what she was experiencing would feel something like a flu and her period rolled into one.

How could it not?

She supposed it was too much to ask that her transformation be painless. Darn it. After her ordeal with the priest, she just wanted to go back home with Ash. To be safe and secure in his arms.

Crazy how a man she'd just met meant so much to her.

Was it too sudden?

Gabby was not one to ponder the validity of love at first sight, and yet, she was pretty sure she was halfway in love with the beautiful Demon after one meeting.

Yes.

Mate.

Mine.

The whispered words were followed by an intense growl and a cramp that almost sent her to the floor. Gabby clutched her abdomen with one hand and opened the passenger side door with the other. She sat down with her feet on the sidewalk. Maybe if she just breathed for a while the cramps would go away. Maybe.

Not likely, something inside of her whispered.

Then she saw it in her mind's eye, standing clear as day. Her she-Wolf. A beautiful caramel colored beast with

long, sharp teeth and piercing blue eyes.
Awoooooo.

CHAPTER ELEVEN

THE ARID AIR felt warm and dry, cooler than what he was used to, and definitely a relief after a gory afternoon spent beating back a horde of soulless rogues. But Ash had no time to enjoy the change of temperature and atmosphere as he exited a portal on his way to meet Gabriella. Something was wrong. He felt a force, unseen but strong, as if he were tethered to something, pulling him in the same direction he'd been heading.

He was early, despite Aphrodite's warning that he would seem desperate. The fact was, Ash was desperate. Shockingly determined to see her, almost to the point of frenzied. He ran his hands through his newly shorn locks. Cutting his shoulder length black hair into a more modern style was another of Aphrodite's suggestions.

"You can't go storming after the woman looking like that, Ashmedai! She'll run for the hills," gasped the goddess after he'd returned from battle with a burning need to find his mate.

Only after catching a glimpse of himself in the mirror had he seen she was right. He'd been covered in filth and gore, his campaign against the soulless a success much to Lucifer's delight and everyone's safety. Typically, he'd celebrate at the bar with a round for his comrades, which was where he'd headed with his legion. Of course, once there, he'd picked up the faint hint of Gabriella's scent on the air and tried to head up the stairs. That was where the Goddess of Love stepped in.

"Oh, no you don't! Dammit, Ash, you will not ruin my reputation for matchmaking by scaring the little Wolf off before she even had time to bone you!"

Yes. She'd used the word *bone.* Which was the only way she'd managed to catch him off guard. A little shocked, he'd allowed himself to be shoved into a shower stall where he dutifully cleaned himself up. After his haircut and shave, he'd dropped by Arachne's shop to pick up a new set of clothes, and here he was. Dressed and at the ready, and bloody damned furious at himself for the time he'd wasted on his appearance when he noticed Gabriella's car sitting on the sidewalk, door ajar, and his scrumptious little female nowhere in sight.

"Hot as hell today, isn't it?" a random passerby said.

"Not really, no," Ash replied, glaring at the suddenly pale man who rushed away.

His own damn fault for speaking before being spoken to, Ash thought rudely. He jogged toward the car, inhaling deeply as he reached the vehicle. She'd been there recently, only moments ago, in fact. He could see her heat signature, read it on the air as easily as a living breathing thermo-imaging camera.

It was another of his Demonic gifts, and one he used to track his prey. Though, he'd never dreamed he'd be hunting his own mate. Another deep inhale and somewhere beneath the familiar vanilla-raspberry-lime fragrance, he discovered the problem.

"Shit. Gabriella, I'm coming," he murmured, taking off at breakneck speeds to follow her trail all the way to the Hermosa Valley Greenbelt trail.

Shit.

This was obviously a popular hiking

destination, he could tell by the joggers and dog walkers in the area. Not a good place for a Werewolf to have her first Change.

"Hold on, Gabriella. I'm coming."

Breaking promises was no way to begin a relationship. Even a Demon knew that much. Ash was already vowing to make it right by the time he caught up to her, doubled over in agony near a tall and shady pine.

"Gabriella!" he yelled.

Her gaze flashed to him, the beautiful blue rimmed in a glowing silver color that was simply beautiful.

Like watching an ocean turn to ice or the sky swallowed by a cloud.

Riveting, breathtaking, and he could not look away. Even as he approached calmly, arms wide, palms up.

She trembled as another wave of pain washed over her, and Ash grunted, feeling it as if it were his own. Gabriella growled deep inside her chest, a sound that spoke to his own Demon who responded with his own guttural reverberation.

"Hurts," she whimpered.

"I know, love. You're fighting it. I can sense your fear," he said, whipping his head back as someone approached.

Thankfully, the jogger was too busy checking his fitness watch to bother with them. Still, he thought, staying there was a recipe for disaster.

"Listen, love, I am going to lift you up. It is going to hurt because you are starting your Change. Your skin is exceedingly sensitive, but we must go somewhere more private. This place is too crowded."

"Okay," she nodded, and he paused.

"Are you sure—"

"Would you ever hurt me, Ash?" Gabriella asked, cutting him off.

Her eyes were glowing full on silver, and he knew he had to move her out of there and fast. But first her question, though it didn't truly seem like one. More like she was forcing him to think about his own hesitations.

"Never! Gabriella, I know things seem crazy and fast, but I swear I would never hurt you," Ash said, his response automatic.

"I know, Ash. I trust you."

Her reply shocked and humbled him.

He had her trust. Nothing had ever felt better to him, except maybe her love. But he could wait for that, he realized, knowing full well he was already in love with her.

Ash swore he saw playfulness in her eyes, and when he looked even deeper, he saw resolve and certitude. If he were a praying Demon, Ash would've dropped to his knees in that moment. As it were, he simply thanked all the gods for the gift of her. Then he hauled ass, attending her needs first was his priority.

The sweet, beautiful miracle that was Gabriella Keen somehow, someway, trusted in him, in Asmodeus, Demon of Lust, Prince of Hell, to do right by her. And she wasn't above letting him see her feelings, despite the obvious pain of her Shift.

No mind games or manipulations. Not with her. She was real and pure and honest, and fuck, he did not deserve her. No. Not in this lifetime.

But he would take her. Ash had every intention of keeping the beautiful she-Wolf as his own. The second she was willing, he planned to gather her close, claim her with his bite, and hold on tightly to her with both hands. For as long as he could, until he took his very last breath.

Forever, his Demonic side inserted.

Mine.

Forever mine.

"Ash," she whispered his name, gorgeous silver orbs boring into his. "I *know* you would never hurt me. I trust you. Please, take me somewhere safe, Ash. Before I scare the crap out of these people, or worse, hurt someone."

His heart squeezed at the sound of Gabriella's voice. Laced with pain and breathy with her pants, it hurt him to hear her this way. He wanted to take away all her hurt, to make her feel good, but he understood, perhaps better than she, that sometimes you had to experience pain to get to what was really good. Still, he'd take it all away if he could. For now, though, he would have to content himself with doing as she bade him.

"I got you, love. It will all be over soon," he said, lifting her into the safety of his arms.

ASH

She sighed, resting her overly warm forehead on his chin, and he felt a tremor rack his entire frame. Fuck, he loved her trust in him. Would do all he could to ensure he was worthy of that one thing that meant more than any other, starting with this.

"Hold on," he growled, ducking back behind the tree line as a group of dogwalkers neared them.

The dogs were barking like mad, some whimpering and whining as they came closer to where they'd been a moment before. The beasts were probably scenting her Wolf. Thankfully, Gabriella was too focused on herself to pay them any mind. Her unsteady breathing another sign that she was fighting too hard.

Fuck.

He had to do something. Go somewhere to make sure she was safe.

But where would a Demon take a new Wolf to Change and run for the first time?

"Ash," she said his name through gritted as the pain gripped her harder than before.

"Hold on."

His only thought of her, Ash used the shadows to travel like lightning to the nearest portal. The Underworld might not be what some would call a vacation spot. But it was home.

And he wanted her there, in his keep, in his house, with him more than anything.

Possessive?

Fuck yes. Unapologetically so. He was a Demon, after all. Not an exceptionally generous being. But he would give everything he had for and to Gabriella. She was it for him.

Mine.

Mine.

MINE.

CHAPTER TWELVE

HOT. SO HOT.

For a woman who always felt chilly, even in LA's desert like heat, Gabby was on fire. She felt the warmth all the way down to her bones. It wasn't cozy or comfortable. Not at all. The burning pain was enough to sear the flesh right off her.

And did she mention the cramps in her muscles?

Holy cow!

Not cursing was an active lifestyle choice, but for once in her life, she didn't think she'd make it without uttering one obscene word.

Was this normal?

Something had to be wrong.

She opened her eyes to find Ash bent over her, concern and patience in his black orbs. He'd brought her here, back to his home, placed her on the center of his bed. She'd asked him not to, afraid she'd damage the thing, but he wouldn't hear of laying her anywhere else.

"You must let your Wolf in, little one," he pleaded. "It will hurt far less if you accept her."

"Burns," she growled and grunted, rolling to her side as pain racked her frame.

"Please, Gabriella, I cannot bear to see you like this. What can I do to help?"

"Stay," she whimpered, the only word that came to mind.

She closed her eyes, trying to breathe through the worst of it. She heard that same strange voice inside her head, pleading and begging to be let out. Only Gabby could not relinquish control of herself. Certainly not to some mythical being. Heck. She didn't even know how.

"Boss?" Ernie's voice penetrated through her haze, and she vaguely heard Ash give the Imp some curt instructions.

"Shouldn't be harsh on him," she scolded, but it was hardly effective, as her whisper was fragile.

"This is not going how it should, Gabriella. I sent Ernie for help."

"I'm sorry I—"

"No! I didn't mean it to sound as if it is your fault—"

Footsteps brought her head up, and she saw Eve and someone else next to her, a strange woman.

Not a woman, her inner voice said.

Wolf.

"Hello, Ash," the woman said, walking into the room. "Eve tells me your name is Gabby, is it? I'm Chloe, and I think I can help."

Gabby tried to smile, but it came out a snarl. Oops. The lovely woman simply raised her eyebrow before stealing a glance at Ash, whose sole focus remained on her. Thank goodness. It was the only thing keeping her from freaking the heck out.

"Alright, listen up, Gabby. Your Wolf was dormant for quite some time, but with the new changes in the supernatural world after the fall of the Curse, she is looking to be freed from that metaphysical plane where she dwells until you call. Now, that's the supernatural science of it. Anyone could've told you that. What I am going to tell you is more personal. Listening?"

Gabby growled, nodding her head. Beads of sweat rolled down the sides of her face, and she arched as another wave of staggering pain struck.

"It's like my insides are being squeezed with vices," she grunted.

ASH

"I know," Chloe frowned, turning to Ash. Gabby was unsure what they were whispering, but she heard a few phrases about something between mates and bonds and giving her strength.

"I would give her everything," Ash replied with a Demonic hiss.

"Good," Chloe said, turning back to Gabby. "She might need it."

"Gabriella, look at me," Ash instructed, and she turned her head, gaze landing on his.

"Good, Gabby. I want you to use Ash as your focal point," Chloe said, her voice had an oddly calming effect that Gabby really, really liked.

"Keep looking at him, Gabby. See him there. He will protect you with his life. Not let anything bad happen. Now close your eyes, see your Wolf? She is part of you. She will protect you too. Trust her. Let her out, Gabby. Your Wolf is part of who you are and, like Ash, she will never lead you astray."

The woman's words were like magic. Or maybe that was the steady assurance she felt flowing from Ash. Either way, Gabby felt the heat inside of her flame to volcanic temperatures, her body arched and a scream tore from her throat. The sound changing midway through to something she'd heard only in nature documentaries.

"Agggghhhhhwwwwooooooooooo!"

Some remnants of cloth stuck to her as she panted in place, but most were torn in the process. Hysteria gone, Gabby glanced around, noting her slightly askew vision. Everything seemed more in focus, and she could see more than just who was there and the room. It was like she could see smells and heat signatures. Her new Wolf's eyes searched for Ash and found him, looking grim but relieved when she walked over to where he stood and nudged him with her lupine nose.

"Gabriella?" he murmured, dropping to his knees, his black eyes glowing obsidian as he raised a hand tentatively.

Warmth rushed through her as his fingertips skimmed her fur. Looking down, she realized her fur was brown with golden tips, and her paws were massive, with huge claws that clicked on the stone flooring of Ash's home. Oh no, her head snapped, and she saw the damage she'd done to his bed.

"Don't worry, Gabby, Ernie is already on it," Chloe said, smiling down at her. "And I apologize for barging in since we weren't properly introduced, but it is nice to meet you. Take care."

With that, the woman left, and Gabriella's focus was back on Ash. Feelings she'd been too afraid to acknowledge as a human seemed so simple, now. It was as if her soul was laid bare, stark and naked for him to see, and for some reason, she wasn't worried or embarrassed.

Mine.

Her Wolfish thoughts were clear and definite. The Demon Ash was hers, and she wanted him in every way. Gabby was too awestruck to be shocked by the carnal turn of her thoughts. Her Wolf seemed eager and ready to mark the male as hers. The animal knew without fail that they were destined.

"So beautiful," Ash whispered as his long fingers wove their way through her fur.

The beast preened at his praise, wanting more, and yet she itched to run, to try out this new body. His eyes flashed and turned to the door. As if he'd read her mind, Ash stood gesturing with a wicked grin that made her bark playfully at the sexy Demon. She wanted a chase.

"Go on then, lady mine. There is a small path that leads to a courtyard directly behind my home. I will follow. You won't get far," he said, opening the door to the Underworld.

Gabby yipped and took off, running harder and harder. Gabriella pushed her suddenly very able body as fast as she could. She ignored the yell coming from behind her, glorying in the newfound strength and freedom she had in this form.

She wasn't poor chubby Gabriella anymore. Not in her fur. Oh no. This Gabby was sleek and cunning, fast and powerful. She liked the feeling. A lot. Maybe that was why she ignored the call of her mate, yes, she recognized him for what he was now, and kept on going. Running full steam until she could go no more.

Passing shops and the quaint little village-like atmosphere of the

Underworld that she barely remembered from the night before, Gabby continued at breakneck speed. She heard wings flap, claws skitter, smelled the faint scent of sulfur and fire beneath it all. It was like her senses had magnified a hundredfold.

Illuminating, breathtaking, and incredible. So many new sensations, too many to name, and Gabby reveled in them. A wall of black thorns spread out before her and she skidded to a stop, panting heavily. Turning her lupine head, she waited for Ash, but she must've lost him somewhere along the way.

No worries.

He would find her.

He'd said as much, and the Wolf that

was her had no reason to disbelieve him. So much to learn, she mused as she put her nose to the black, ashy covered ground and sniffed lightly. Weird. There was no scent. Like someone had cleaned the area, cleared it of any remnant or trace of existence.

The rest of the Underworld she'd seen zooming by on her wild journey was a thriving town, this was not. There was a dark and dangerous feel to the area just beyond the thorn forest.

Something lurked there.

Something *wrong*.

Gabby snarled. Her Wolfish lip pulled back to reveal enormous fangs. She could see her own reflection in one of the puddles that appeared just in front of her. Her enormous caramel brown Wolf looked fierce and proud, and she was careful not to step one paw in the black liquid.

"Gabriella!" Ash shouted from behind her, and she barked once to alert him of her location.

Ash rushed to her side. His spicy sandalwood scent filling her sensitized nostrils. Immediately, she calmed. As if simply being near him was enough to settle her nerves. But she was still aware of something not quite right about the place.

"Never do that again," her Demon mate muttered, dropping to his knees and embracing her.

Nice, but could be better.

No sooner had the thought emerged then she felt an electrical hum wash over her limbs. It was not painful. Not like before, but she recognized the magical sensation and this time, when her bones began to break and re-knit themselves, Gabriella allowed the sensations to wash over her as they were meant to.

"Ash," she sighed, naked as the day she was born, and wrapped her arms around his neck, pressing her mouth to his.

Passion flared to life, though, in her case, it had never really waned. She moaned, opening her lips, and pressing her tongue into his mouth. She'd never been the aggressor, and yet, with him she couldn't deny her feelings, her desires. Every fiber of her being pushed her closer into his arms.

ASH

"Gabriella," he murmured her name, arms wrapped tightly around her followed by his large, black, leathery wings.

"Take me home," she whispered, kissing his cheek, then his chin, and his neck.

His hands tightened on her flesh, and she loved the sting of his claws. He was losing control of his Demon, as if she was somehow testing his limits with her unpracticed kisses and words.

Yesss, she thought as his hardened manhood pressed into her soft belly. Knowing she'd done that to him made her proud, bold, and she ran her hands down his muscled chest and sleek abs to the long, hard length of him beneath his slacks. Need fueled her desire. It felt so good, so right to touch him.

Call her mad. Call her nuts. She didn't care. She was meant to do this. It was as if she was seeing clearly for the first time, and her vision was full of him.

Her soul mate.

Yes, something inside her confirmed the sentiment.

She was born for this. Made to be with him, to touch and kiss this man, this Demon. She wanted to give herself to him freely and without hesitation.

Yes.

Now.

Gabby wanted to be with Ash more than anything.

To belong to him.

To be his and his alone.

It shocked her, those feelings of

possession that burned within. Shocked and delighted her. So many people walked around oblivious to their true desires, and here she was, feeling every one of them for the truth they were.

Ash was her destiny. Even a timid Sunday school teacher could not deny that.

Why should she?

Especially when every fiber of her being was pressing her to seal the deal.

Claim.

Mate.

Mine.

"Now, Ash," Gabby said firmly.

"Take me home, now."

CHAPTER THIRTEEN

MINE. MINE. MINE.

The word pounded through his brain like an ancient drum beating tattoo across time itself. The Demon of Lust was brought to his knees, at the mercy of one single woman.

Someone call the fucking papers, he thought with a self-deprecating grin.

"Now, Ash," she said firmly. *"Take me home, now."*

His still unmated female spurned him into action with her strongly uttered command, and he was helpless to resist.

Why the fuck would he even want to?

"Yesssss," he hissed his reply.

Shit.

He hadn't almost lost control of himself like this since he was new to the universe. His kind was not exactly born, and yet, he felt like a child. Like he was experiencing everything for the first time. And with her at his side, he was.

"I need you, Gabriella," he whispered his confession, and the responding look in her luminous blue eyes said everything. It said it all.

When he'd met her, during a speed

dating event run by Aphrodite and Eve, Ash was afraid the mostly human female would refuse him. After all, his world was not hers. But she'd taken it all remarkably well. Offering to help her through her Change was an excuse to be with her. Though, of course, he wanted to help.

And now, here she was, willing and wanting, and in his arms. His soul was calling out to her, and miracle of miracles, hers was answering.

What glorious mercy had gifted him such a chance to be happy as this?

He'd certainly never expected it. But Ash was not one to look a gift horse in the mouth.

Her sweet, seductive scent was heady and enticing. That crisp raspberry lime mixed with a woody vanilla warmth that he was dying to experience straight from the source.

"Hold on," he growled, every inch of him attuned to his female.

So attuned, in fact, Ash missed the pair of glowing eyes watching from beyond the thorny expanse of bushes that warned Purgatory dwellers they were too close to the border.

Having her there with him was too much for his senses. He needed to possess her. Wanted to claim her. Was dying to sink into the heaven that awaited him between her perfectly thick thighs.

"Ashhhhh," she whimpered, pressing her lush body firmly against his while she nuzzled his jaw and neck, sending all available oxygen south of his belt buckle.

Fuuucckk.

"Hurry."

He didn't have to be told twice. Moving through shadows was something not every Demon was gifted with, but Ash was very old and very powerful. The urgency with which he found himself moving would have created quite the scene had he not slipped into shadow at the end of town, only to reemerge just outside his own back door.

"Boss? Can I help the good mistress?" Ernie scuttled toward them.

The Imp quickly turned around, a small squeak of surprise escaped his mouth as he shielded his vision from the sight of Ash's naked mate wrapped around him.

Smart.

Very smart.

"Go home, Ernie. We won't be needing you," Ash growled, tucking his wings back into the shadow realm while Gabby started unbuttoning buttons and tugging on his belt.

"Yes, boss!" Ernie said, scrambling away.

Ash heard the approval in his servant's voice but paid it no mind. His heart was racing, palms sweating, and everything in him was focused on one ultimate goal.

To claim Gabriella.

Here.

Now.

And for always.

Her hands worked together with his, and Ash was undressed in under a minute. Still, it was too long to be separated from her. Burning need rose, engulfing him swiftly in an inferno of desire. He reveled in the flames licking at his skin as he nudged Gabriella down onto the new mattress and sheets Ernie had so quickly provided.

Good Imp.

He deserves a raise.

Ash would ensure it. Later though. Much, much later.

"Ash," his mate whispered his name, whimpering as his hands brushed over her silken skin tentatively, reverently.

He wanted to memorize every smooth inch of her. To commit even the smallest detail, every nuance of her physique, to his eternal memory. So soft. So beautiful.

"Gabriella," he growled deep in his throat.

Her name was lovely too. *It suits her*, he thought as she lifted herself onto her knees, hands on his shoulders as she pressed her sweet, soft form to his muscular chest. Ash hissed at the contact, swallowing her responding moan as he crashed his mouth to hers.

He wanted to woo her. Should have been able to, given his extensive history. But for the first time in his life, the Demon of Lust was rendered undone by this sweet, mostly human vixen. Like a virgin, Ash's hands trembled as he took her in his arms, swallowing her exquisite flavors with every lap of his tongue against hers.

"More," he growled, insatiable for her.

Ash pressed his lips to her ear, her neck, licking a trail to her collarbone and down to the rounded perfection of her breasts. Gabriella moaned, hands clutching his hair as she threw her head back, lips parted. She was so fucking beautiful. It almost hurt to look at her, but nothing could make him close his eyes or turn away from her.

Neither wild horses, nor hordes of the soulless could force his eyes away. No force in the universe could make him stop gazing at the only woman in the world who owned him body, heart, mind, and soul. His need was immeasurable. And even greater was the desire to please her.

ASH

Gabriella.

Mine, his Demon whispered in a deep, guttural voice.

Possession pulsed through him. The need to claim, to become one with her so great, he thought he'd perish without her.

But he would not rush. And he would never, ever force. Gabriella was everything to him, now. She would always have the last say. And as Ash's focus remained firmly on her, he continued to kiss, lick, and suckle her sweet and swollen nipples. All the while his hands traced her plentiful curves, reveling in the sumptuous flare of her hip, the petal soft skin of her inner thighs as he traced small patterns on her flesh, forging a trail to her most secret place.

"Yesssss," he hissed as his fingertips delved between her slick folds.

She was wet and hot, so hot, for him. The knowledge had his cock throbbing, jutting forward, desperate to enter her tight heat. Ash was no stranger to carnal pleasures, but nothing compared to his making love to his one true and fated mate.

Nothing on Heaven, Earth, Hell, or Purgatory.

Nor on any of the planes in between.

"Mine," he grunted, settling himself between her thick thighs.

Gabriella panted, her hips rocked gently, trying to entice him closer. But he needed a moment. Had to take the time to simply appreciate the beauty of her womanhood.

"Look at you, my love. So pink and perfect. Can't wait to taste you. Can't wait to make you come," he growled, nuzzling her lips with his nose and tongue.

"Oh please, Ash, please," she begged, rocking her hips a little harder.

He grinned, holding her still with two hands on her hips. His mouth watered at the tiny little taste he'd permitted himself.

But it was not enough.

Not nearly.

Unable to wait any longer, he leaned forward, his tongue snaked out of his mouth, and finally, he tasted her from her forbidden rosette to her tiny, swollen clit. Again and again he stroked her, using the flat of his long tongue. And fuck, how she loved it.

"Ash!" she screamed his name, moaning and panting, pulling his hair as he increased his pace.

Faster, harder, longer, he fucked her with his mouth, refusing to slow down or use any other bit of him. Ash grabbed onto her hips, holding her nice and steady, nudging her legs farther apart. He speared her with his tongue.

Growling at the intense pleasure he felt in pleasuring her. Fuck, she was so hot. Her needy little pants and moans nearly his undoing. His dick ached to be buried inside her.

But he wouldn't give in.

Not until she came.

Everything else was second place to

that one goal. She would come. And she would come hard, or he'd die trying. And Ash had no intention of dying save for the Medieval version between her gorgeous legs.

"Oh god, Ash, no more, can't take it, can't—"

"You can, love. Come for me. Then I'll fill you, ease the ache here, want that?" Ash asked as he cupped her mound, loving the way she moaned and nodded her head. Then he closed his mouth over her clit, and he sucked. Hard.

"Ahh!" With a roar-like scream, Gabriella came. He swallowed every drop of her raspberry lime honey, kissing his way back up to her mouth while his engorged cock pressed inside her.

Slowly, feeding her an inch of his

swollen cock at a time, Ash kissed Gabriella's eyelids. Loving the way she responded, body opening, face turning toward him, her own mouth seeking his, he was in no rush. For the first time ever, the Demon of Lust wanted to give more than he wanted to take.

"Gabriella, mine," he moaned, kissing her chin, her cheek, the corner of her mouth.

"Oh god," she whimpered as he gave her another, then another inch.

"So good, my love. You feel perfect," he confessed, sliding all the way to the hilt.

Ash stilled, allowing her a moment to adjust to his size and girth. The pleasure of being seated deep inside his mate was second to none. Joy radiated through him, wonder and sheer happiness never felt before. His black eyes locked onto hers, then he began to move.

Ash knew then, nothing was ever going to be the same. His thick cock sheathed in her tight channel like a perfectly fitted glove. The deep, steady pace he set had sweat beading on his brow, and his focus intent on every nuance of response from her.

Gabriella was sublime in her submission. She opened and accepted every thrust and flex, cradling him in her heat with an open willingness that stole his breath. Ash had never felt such intense passion, such pure unadulterated bliss, and all because of her, his sweet Gabriella.

Mine.

Mate.

No one knew better than he the many facets of lovemaking, but Ash would swear before any and all that his sweet, sultry mate taught him things he'd never known were even possible. Every sigh, each breathy moan dragged from her sweet lips was a reward for his efforts, and he doubled, tripled them, wanting more of her headlong response.

"Please," she begged, and he obliged, giving her everything he could, all he had.

How could he not?

All he wanted to do was give her pleasure, to show her how much he loved her with his body. He worked her hard and fast, readying for the moment when she first shattered around him.

Fuck, he could hardly breathe with wanting her.

Her walls tightened, gripping his shaft like a velvet vise. Gabriella's nails raked down his back, the sweet bite of pain making this, his claiming her, all the more erotic. Ash was lost in sensation, even as he felt his fangs descend and his wings and tail ripple in and out of this plane of existence.

"Need you to come, my love. Need it now so that I may claim you," he growled, his voice so deep and guttural he barely recognized it himself.

His Demon urged him on. The dark beast within him urging him to take her harder, faster, deeper. To claim her with his mating mark and complete the bond they had begun simply by meeting. For the first time since his chat with Lucifer, Ash entertained the idea that he was destined for a mate. More than entertained, he knew it without a doubt.

Gabriella Keen was his.

His one and true fated mate.

"Yes, yes," Gabriella replied, as if she read his mind. Maybe she was. Beads of sweat dotted her brow as she clung to his shoulders and wrapped her legs tightly around his waist.

With a passionate snarl, Ash took her waist as he rose to his knees, lifting her with him. He pressed her back into the cushioned headboard, flexing, circling, plunging into her with quick, hard, deft movements. Holding onto his own ecstasy was almost impossible, but he managed, up until he felt the first wave of orgasm ripple through her sumptuous body.

"Mine. You're mine, sweet Gabriella, always," he growled, and struck, biting her on the neck and sealing her fate as his one and only.

Possessive much?

Fuck yes.

Pleasure howled through his veins as Ash growled and swallowed down her sweet blood. He took three pulls on her neck, sealing the matebond firmly between them. He would have no doubts, no halfway claims. No way. Gabriella was his. Even if he had to fight all of Heaven and Hell for her, he would.

Licking the puncture marks closed, Ash grunted, hips still pumping as she climaxed again, his name spilling from her open lips. His own orgasm tore through him, increasing in strength and endurance with the sudden burst of pain that erupted from his left shoulder.

Holy fuck.

She has staked her claim!

Pleasure erupted like the tide, washing over and through him like nothing he'd ever felt. The sight of her head bowed, and her mouth around his flesh as she gifted him with her bite was something Ash had never dreamed would happen.

She claimed him back!

The gorgeous she-Wolf had bitten him. Gifting him with her mating mark.

Him.

The Demon of Lust.

A Prince of Hell.

Pride and bliss raced through his veins until he felt as if his heart would explode.

Ash was alone no more. His whole life he'd believed himself cursed and doomed, but this creature, this beautiful, miraculous woman, had proved him wrong. Gabriella Keen was so much more than Wolf and woman.

She was his savior.

His reason.

His everything.

She was his mate.

Asmodeus' mate.

And he was never letting go.

She was his now, and he was hers. Their matebond pulsed around them, wrapping them in a cocoon of power and heat that seared the very flesh on his bones.

For the first time, he was not alone. For the first time, he belonged to someone.

He belonged to her.

Gabriella Keen.

His mate.

Mine.

Always.

CHAPTER FOURTEEN

GABRIELLA STRETCHED HER deliciously sore muscles and sighed as she slowly came awake. She felt magnificent.

Go figure, her inner Wolf snarked, and though their connection was new, she knew the beast was pleased.

Just as she knew that last night was

the kind of life-altering sex she'd only ever read about prior to meeting him.

Her mate.

The word felt foreign, and yet it was the right one. She was certain of that. Just as she was certain she could hear someone, Ernie, scuttling about somewhere in the other rooms of Ash's vast home.

Speaking of her mate, where was he?

She sat up, her hand going right for the warm spot he left right beside her. Her Wolf rose to the forefront and Gabby inhaled, sifting through the various flavors in the bedroom until she found his. The spicy dark fragrance seemed to permeate the very walls of the house and her Wolf barked happily, more than satisfied to be breathing her mate in.

"Good morning," a deep, familiar voice startled her, and she gasped, turning to see Ash walking toward her with a breakfast tray in his hands, and nothing else covering his magnificent frame.

She licked her lips, gaze roaming over every inch of the perfect male in front of her. He was beautiful, perfectly proportioned, and then some. Like he was carved from marble at the hands of a master. And all for her.

Mine.

"Yours," he echoed her thoughts, eyes bleeding to black as he placed the tray on the nightstand and took her face in his hands.

Ash pressed his mouth to hers and Gabby responded on instinct, opening for him, and taking from him as much as he was willing to give. She wanted to drown in his kiss, to get lost in his arms, and never, ever find her way back. Her feelings were so intense she damn near fell off the bed as they raced through her mind.

"Easy love," he whispered, kissing her more gently and turning to hand her a cup of steaming hot coffee. "Here you are."

"Thanks," she whispered, sipping the warm drink, and hoping it would fortify her.

She wasn't normally one of those women taken to flights of fancy or love at first sight, but what she felt for Ash was real. So real, it scared her.

"I know what you mean," he

whispered, lifting his own mug to his lips.

"Can you read my mind?"

"Sort of," he grinned. "It's like I can hear part of you inside, but I think that's because you're projecting your feelings to me."

"That's not fair," she said, smiling, though it freaked her out a bit.

I am just as vulnerable, my love.

Gabby gasped. She'd heard his words clear as a bell, but his lips were currently occupied as he drank from his mug. He replaced it on the tray and took her hands, smiling at her shocked surprise.

"It is all part of the matebond," he explained.

"You are my mate," she whispered,

awestruck by the fact.

Her chest warmed at the announcement. The steady thudding of that wondrous muscle beat inside of her, seeming to hasten at the mere thought of him. Gabby closed her eyes, trying to get a hold of her emotions. It was all so fast, but last night, right now, it all felt so very right.

"I know, love. I have had over a thousand years on this plane. I have been aware of the miracle of fated mates, and yet all that time and knowledge could not have prepared me for the reality. Truth is, I've never felt anything like this."

"Me either. Is it crazy? I mean, should we slow down?"

"Do you want to slow down?" Ash

asked, head cocked to the side.

Gabby giggled and lifted a piece of perfectly cooked bacon to her mouth.

"I suppose that would be like trying to put a lid on a hurricane."

"I think you might be right," he replied, eyes twinkling.

"So, is this what you meant by mates?"

Ash stilled at her prodding question, but she had to know. Needed to have her own suspicions validated with words. Maybe that was her human side talking, after all, the she-Wolf seemed to feel it without words.

"Yes, love," he replied with a quiet intensity she felt echoing inside her own heart. "You are my fated mate, Gabriella. Last night, we claimed one another with our bites. Our bond is strong, unbreakable, my love. I know it seems fast, but the feelings I have for you—"

"I have them too," she replied, cutting him off.

Happiness bloomed in the bedroom as they chatted and ate. It was wonderfully intimate and yet felt as natural to Gabby as breathing. After they finished, he led her to the shower, adjusting the knobs until the water reached the perfect temperature.

"Come here," Ash said, a wicked grin on his handsome face.

His skin glowed like alabaster as he stepped backward into the spray of water. The hot liquid sluiced over his shoulder, running over his muscular frame like loving hands. He did not have to beckon to her twice. Gabby was more than willing to follow him.

"How's the water?" he asked, kissing her cheek and nuzzling her neck as his hands gently skimmed her body.

"Mmm," she whispered, hardly able to form words when he was touching her like that.

For a Sunday school teacher, Gabby had hidden depths to her passion that she'd never been aware of. At least not until Ash brought them out of her. Whether it was his sheer skill, or the fact she was already head over heels in love with the Demon that made their lovemaking so sweet, she had no idea.

All she really knew was if he stopped doing what he was doing right then, she'd turn into a puddle of goo at his feet. He had a way of turning her inside out with a mere caress, a simple slide of skin on skin, and mouth on flesh.

Please don't stop.

Her body shivered with anticipation. The promise of his touch fanning the flames of her need for him until she was whimpering with it. Gabby gasped aloud as his long tongue twirled around one taut nipple. The talented appendage lavished attention on one then the other breast until she was pulling on his hair, wanting him everywhere at once. Ash dropped to his knees in front of her, worshipping her like she was some kind of goddess.

"You are my goddess, sweet. I want to worship you. Let me," he begged, suckling at her breast while his hands spread her legs apart, allowing him access to her molten heat.

Gabby whimpered at the first brush of his thumb over her clit. Already soaked and desperate for him, she moaned aloud when he pierced her core with two thick fingers, circling the tiny nubbin the entire time. Clutching his head to her breast, she leaned against the cool tile, loving the way it felt in contrast to the warm water and Ash's scorching attentions.

The sensual assault was almost too much as his tongue and teeth nibbled and laved their way to her core. Ash growled, lifting one of her legs and draping it over his shoulder.

"Mine," he grunted, leaning forward to feast on her soaked pussy.

"Ash!" Gabby squealed, pulling on his hair.

Or was it pushing?

Gods knew she wanted him closer. She wondered if he was reading her mind then as he started sucking on her clit with enthusiasm, and thrusting his fingers deeper, harder, faster inside her.

Damn, it felt so good.

Every nerve ending was wound tight, waiting for release. But at the same time, she did not want this to end. Gabby had never felt so desired, so beautiful, not in all her life. There was something about always being the chubby, nerdy girl that had her settling in the past. When she was younger, more impressionable, but never again. She would never settle for anything. Not when she had a mate who loved her so well.

I do love you, Gabriella, Ash's voice whispered into her mind.

I will do anything for you.

Give you anything, my mate.

Anything at all.

Love you.

So much.

Love. Love. LOVE.

"I love you too," she moaned as the first wave of her orgasm came crashing over her.

"Yes," Ash growled, rising to his feet and lifting her in the process.

He had hold of her hips, carrying her weight as if she were light as a feather and trusting the wall to keep her back upright. Gabriella trusted him. She knew he wouldn't let her fall. Clutching his wet shoulders, she licked her lips.

"Want you," she said. "Need you, my love. My mate."

That was all she was able to say before Ash rendered her speechless. Eyes fully black, her gorgeous Demon mate growled a deep and guttural sound that struck a chord deep within her. Next, he flexed his hips, spearing her on his hard, long cock.

Oh damn, that felt good.

So good.

She wanted him slow and deep, hard and fast, any way she could get him. She wanted him over and over again. Now, later, and again after that. Gabby wanted Ash. She would never stop wanting him.

"Mate," he growled, driving into her

center, brushing his pubis against her sensitive clit with unerring accuracy with each and every stroke of his engorged cock.

"Yes. Mate," she echoed, feeling the word deep down for the truth it was.

She was his mate. Her Wolf howled in her mind's eye with the knowledge. The beast gloried in belonging to him. Ash was her one and only, the male destined for her by the universe itself.

Chosen by the Fates.

And as she spiraled into ecstasy, Gabby couldn't help a bark of laughter, moaning with delight as he followed her soon after into bliss.

"What's so funny?" Ash asked as he carried her back to their bed wrapped in a fluffy white towel.

"Hmm?"

"You laughed," he stated, dropping her on the mattress and kissing her neck until she giggled and writhed beneath him.

"Oh," she sighed when he finished torturing her. "I was just thinking, here you are, a thousand year old Demon, and I'm just this schoolteacher who found out I'm a Werewolf. But here we both are, Fated mates and all. It's just funny."

"What's funny?"

"Well, I mean, destiny decided we were meant to be, but we had to meet at speed dating," she said, giggling against his shoulder.

One of Ash's eyebrows rose as he contemplated her statement and for a second, she was worried he'd be offended. Then he laughed, and she laughed too, relieved he wasn't angry.

"Oh no," he said sitting up after they were done giggling like teenagers.

"What?"

"Aphrodite and Eve are going to be incorrigible after this," he said, hugging her close to his side.

"Is that bad?"

"Not bad. Just annoying. They're going to want favors now. Probably think I owe them something," he grumbled.

"And don't you? I mean, aren't I worth it?" she teased.

"Yes, of course, love," he replied without hesitation.

Good Demon.

"I am a very good Demon. Now, what

did you want to do today?"

"I have a few ideas," she said, straddling his waist.

And for a Sunday school teacher, her ideas were really quite something.

Mine.

CHAPTER FIFTEEN

ASH GROWLED AS he walked into the Guard. He eyed a few legates lounging lazily against the wall with mugs of coffee until one actually dropped his. Fuckers should at least pretend to look busy when their General was in the building.

"What news of the southern borders?"

he asked.

"Nothing, General. It's been quiet going on thirty-six hours."

"I see. Have Legion six do a sweep of the area and get back to me with their progress. I will be in my office," he grunted, nodding at the Imp who was busy cleaning up the legate's spilled coffee.

Imbeciles.

He was out of sorts, cranky really, and he knew the reason. He would much rather be at home, committing every inch of his gorgeous mate to memory, but duty called. Besides, Gabriella was topside at the moment. He took her to get some things from her stepmother's house packed, then he was picking her up in a few hours and bringing her back to their home.

Ash still could not believe how very lucky he was that his mate chose him. The fact she'd given him her bite mark still made him shiver with delight and pride. He only wished it were higher on his neck so that everyone could see it.

Hmm.

Maybe he would ask her to do it again later.

Grrrr.

"Sir, we've been tracking this band of rogues after the roundup the other night. We destroyed many, but it seems these few got away. They've abandoned their attempts to breach security of the southern borders," Dell, legate of the seventh cohort to the Southlands, spoke up.

"Really? That is interesting. Can we tell where they went?"

"Yes, sir. Seems they went topside. I suppose that makes them someone else's problem then, eh, General?" Dell smirked.

"Where are they, exactly?"

Ash stood up, hands gripping his desk so tightly he felt the stone crumble beneath the force. His heart stopped beating while he waited for his legate to confirm his worst fears. The band of soulless had gone topside.

Straight to Hermosa Beach.

"Gabriella!" He snarled and vaulted over the desk.

"I want all legions on deck now. Send double the troops to the Southlands. They have not abandoned their efforts.

They are merely trying to distract me by threatening my mate," he shouted as he ran to the nearest portal.

"Mate? Boss?" Dell asked, but Ash snarled over his shoulder, and the Demon bowed low, his hands rapidly moving over his tablet, already doing Ash's bidding.

Good.

At least he didn't have to kill the fucker.

Panic had him shoving past the Sphinx, who uttered a rude word only to bite her tongue when Ash's tail whipped out and smacked her on the forehead.

The Demon was in no mood.

He wanted his mate.

Now.

At his nod, the Sphinx initiated the

portal and Ash emerged, barely able to cloak his wings and horn in time. A necessary, though annoying, evil when walking in the human world.

Was he too late?

He hated to even think it.

"Gabriella!" Ash bellowed her name as he used the shadows to travel to her door, panic holding him tightly in its grip.

He smelled the sulfuric stink of the soulless and recognized the soot covered claw prints that marked the grass in the yard leading up to her bedroom window. The sound of glass shattering sped him on, and Ash roared as he crashed through the half broken orifice to see Gabriella half-shifted and holding one soulless off the ground by the throat.

Holy fuck!

His mate was fearsome and strong, her caramel fur bursting from her pores as she used her Shifter powers to protect herself. Ash bared his fangs at the rogue who dared trespass on the human plane. Another lay gutted on the floor, his carcass already crackling and turning to dust. There was a third struggling beneath his foot, but Ash simply pressed harder. He'd landed on the foul creature when he burst into the room.

"Gabriella! Are you okay?"

His mind raced as his gaze roamed over her body. She had scratches and her clothes were torn in places, but he guessed that was more from her half-shift than the bastards who'd dared harmed her. He was torn wanting to rejoice at the joy he felt at the fact she was all right and needing to lay waste to the whole fucking lot of soulless. The bastards dared touch what was his!

Gabby growled, unable to speak with her half-changed face. He nodded, he understood, but he could not help being distracted by the scent of more of her blood. The bastard she was holding had dared strike out with his claws!

Without wasting another moment, Ash leapt into action, smiting the creature beneath his heel with a sharp stab to its forehead with Ash's tail.

As if she understood his intentions, Gabby tossed the rogue she'd held by the throat and Ash struck him next. His poisoned venom did its work instantaneously. The second he struck, both rogues crumbled into soot, leaving piles of dust and a faint stink in the air. Still, it was nothing a good vacuuming and some air freshener couldn't do away with.

He had more important things to worry about at the moment. Like the health and well-being of his mate.

"Gabby!"

Ash waited for her to shift back to human. He gathered her in his arms the second he could without hurting her. The transformation always left Shifters a little sensitive the first few seconds. He had to hold himself in check in order not to grab. But he would never hurt her. Not for anything.

"Did you see that? Wow!" she exclaimed, sounding somewhat gleeful at the gory turn of events.

Ash frowned, unsure if she was truly all right or if it was just shock talking.

"I am so sorry, my love. This should never have happened. I think some of these rogues must have followed us the other day when you ran to the borders of Purgatory," he explained, but she was shaking her head.

"Really? Wow! Well, I have never had so much fun."

"What?"

Ash stilled.

Was this real?

Was his mate really not upset or threatening to run back to her human life?

He'd been so terrified she'd been hurt, or worse, by the soulless bastards who'd tracked her back to her human home. Second to those fears was the distinct worry that she would realize the danger he put her in, and she would leave him.

Selfish?

Maybe.

But he could not help it. Ash had only just found her. He could not lose her so quickly.

"Hey, look at me," she commanded. "I am not going anywhere. I mean, did you see me? I was like half-woman, half-Wolf, and I totally kicked butt!"

"Yes, you did." Ash grinned back.

She was really something else, his wonderful mate! Gorgeous and sexy, even if she didn't curse and read the Bible for fun. She was still the most badass female he'd ever seen. And she was all his.

How'd a Demon get so lucky?

"Hey! What's all the noise?" Gabriella's stepmother came running into the room.

The older she-Wolf's hair was in a towel, and she was wearing a gaudy red satin robe. But that was nothing compared to her open-mouthed stare at the mess that was once Gabriella's room. She turned, gaping at the pair of them and the piles of dust that sat on the otherwise polished floor.

"Mim! You met Ash, right? But I don't think I introduced you to him yet as my mate." Gabriella smiled, seeming to notice his reticence.

She tugged him forward. She was

oblivious of her own torn clothes where her Wolfish form had ripped through, or the remnants of blood, hers and the soulless, that stained them. Pride welled inside of him as she stood tall and confident and introduced him to her stepmother.

The older woman took in the mess casually. She narrowed her eyes at Ash, measuring him from head to foot, ignoring his wings, tail, and horns, much to his shock. With her hands on her hips, Mim frowned at him and raised one perfectly plucked eyebrow.

"So, you're the man my daughter has taken as a mate," she said, crossing her arms.

"Yes, ma'am. I am Ashmedai, but you can call me Ash. Gabriella and I have sealed our matebond, fated as it were," he stated with quiet pride.

"I see," Mim replied.

"Mim! Be nice!" Gabriella hissed.

"I'll be nice in a minute, dear," Mim said to his mate before turning back to him. "But first, I have a question for him."

"Ask me anything, but know this, I love Gabriella and I will do everything I can in my power to ensure she is safe and happy for the rest of our lives," Ash said, hoping to stem some of the third degree he was expecting from the woman who was essentially his mother-in-law.

Gabby squeezed his hand and smiled, her blue eyes shining like two cornflowers in full bloom under a July sun. She was so beautiful. Ash's chest swelled with joy, and he realized he loved her more than he could have ever imagined.

"Eyes up here, mister," Mim said, snapping her fingers to regain his attention.

He kissed Gabby's hand and turned back to the older Wolf, waiting for her to get on with it. Ash had a powerful urge to get his mate back home so he could strip off the rest of her clothing to ensure she was whole after her ordeal. Okay, so maybe he wanted to do more than that. Maybe he wanted to claim her all over again.

Yes.

Yes, that.

As soon as this woman was finished with her questions, he was going to take his sweet Gabriella home and show her everything he felt for her. He nodded, hoping to hurry her along. Ready to give the woman whatever assurance she needed before he carried her daughter off to the Underworld with him. His cock stiffened beneath his trousers just thinking of his mate's welcoming heat. But first he had to get her out of here, and that meant answering her Mim's inquiries.

Of course, nothing could have prepared him for the words that came out of her mouth. Just as he worried whether his hard on was noticeable, his dick went soft at the other female's question.

Gulp.

"I'm sorry. What?" Ash asked,

uncertain if he heard her correctly.

"I said, when are you going to bring the grandchildren to see me now that you're moving my Gabby to Hell? I think every week might suffice..."

"What?" Gabby asked, her hands moving to cover her abdomen. "Mim, are you sure?" his mate asked with wonder.

"Of course, I am sure! I could scent it the second I saw you. Is he alright?"

Mim pointed to Ash, unaware he'd backed up a step, then two.

Grandchildren?

But she couldn't be?

Could she?

One deep inhale told him the truth of it.

She could be.

She was.

ASH

"OMG! Ash? Ash!" Gabby squeaked his name, but he could hardly reply.

He felt his mate's pleasure and her worry just before the lights went out.

CHAPTER SIXTEEN

LUCIFER STOOD LOOKING tall and proud with his mate on his arm just before he proclaimed Ash and Gabriella as man and wife.

"You may now kiss the bride," the Lord of Purgatory shouted, and Ash was more than happy to oblige.

He lifted the gauzy veil that covered

his mate's beautiful face, revealing her perfect pink smile and cornflower blue eyes as she gazed up at him with love shining in their depths. Ash's hands shook as he held the sheer fabric carefully, though knowing Arachne's skill it was hardly breakable.

"Well, kiss her already!" someone shouted and Gabby giggled briefly before he closed his lips over hers, giving the finger to whoever had dared rush him.

The Underworld erupted into a round of thunderous applause as Ash claimed his new wife's lips. Eve and Aphrodite cheered louder than most, perhaps cause of their nearness serving as maids of honor to his cherished bride. He could almost hear them now, touting their marriage as all due to their Wednesday night speed dating scheme.

Who knew?

Maybe it was.

"I love you," Gabriella said, ending their kiss and nuzzling his cheek with hers.

"I love you too, sweet."

"Are we going to just stand here, or are we going to party?" Lucifer shouted to the throng.

The resounding cheers of those gathered agreed. Almost everyone was there, save for a few legions he'd ordered to patrol the borders. After those few rogues had followed Gabby home, the Daemonium Guard had been on the mission to hunt down the leaders of the soulless uprising.

Many had been captured and

sentenced to dust by Lucifer himself. The safety of Purgatory was paramount to Ash, especially now that he was mated, married, and expecting. He'd learned that most things were a work in progress, but he would never gamble with the future of his mate and family.

"I suppose we better join the reception," Ash said mournfully.

The idea was not exactly unpleasant. It was just, well, he would much rather take his mate back to their house.

Alone.

"I guess so," Gabriella replied with a playful sigh.

"You look beautiful," he murmured, kissing her cheek. "I am dying to peel this dress off of you."

"Mmm, well, don't worry, my love,

soon," Gabby said, squeezing his hand as they walked to the enormous tent erected in the center of town for their celebration.

"Happy?" Ash asked, giving voice to his only real concern. He wanted her happy that she'd chosen him. Hell, he would do anything to ensure it.

"When we get home, I have every intention of showing you just how happy I am," his sweet mate replied.

Then, naughty little minx that she was, she tugged on his arm and whispered in his ear. Ash sucked in a breath while she told him all the delightfully dirty and lusty things she intended to do.

Holy hell.

She certainly was inventive!

ASH

Ash could not contain his growl. Thank fuck his trousers seemed to magically lend room where he suddenly needed it most.

"I thought I was marrying a staid little Sunday school teacher," he said to her robust laughter. "More like a minx!"

"You bring it out in me, my love," she replied with a sexy wink that made his cock grow even harder and his mouth water.

"Later," he growled, tucking her close to his side. "You promise?"

"Yes."

"I can't wait."

"Me either."

If Ash had any doubts that his schoolteacher Werewolf would be happy with a Demon in the Underworld,

Gabriella laid all his fears to rest that night. And as they slept together in a tangle of arms and legs, Ash's hand rested over the slight swell of her stomach where his babe grew peacefully, and he felt their matebond wrap around them in a protective cocoon of love and happiness. One he never wanted to leave.

Mate.

His inner Demon growled, and Ash sighed happily. Yes, he had found his mate, and he was going to hold on to her for eternity.

The end.

Thanks for reading!

Follow our Facebook page here: Speed Dating with the Denizens of the Underworld Series

& learn more about C.D. Gorri here.

Watch your favorite online retailer for the other books in the Speed Dating with the Denizens of the Underworld series.

Turn the page now for an excerpt from *Azrael by Carrie Pulkinen,* Book Three in the Speed Dating with the Denizens of the Underworld series!

EXCERPT

Can the Grim Reaper find life in the undead?

"LOOK AT ME, flirting with Death." Deirdre walked by Azrael's side up the trail, the dry, packed earth having no effect on her high heels. In fact, she moved so smoothly, he wondered if her feet even touched the ground. She had the grace of a feline with a contagious energy that excited him in more ways than one.

As they reached the top of the hill, her breath caught. A single swing hung from a towering tree, overlooking an expanse of the city below. Lights from the houses twinkled like stars in the darkness, disappearing into the horizon and making it hard to tell where Earth ended and the heavens began.

She released his hand to clutch the ropes holding the swing. "What a view."

He stood behind her. "I hope you're not afraid of heights."

"We're not that high."

"Not yet." He unfurled his wings, stretching them outward to their full twelve-foot span.

She spun around, and her eyes widened as she took them in. "You're not suggesting we go flying, are you?"

He hesitated, but he knew what he was doing when he brought her up here. He couldn't back out now, so opened his arms. "I am. Have you ever flown before?"

"Never." Her gaze traveled down his body before returning to his eyes. "I don't suppose you have a magical harness in your pocket? How will I keep from falling?"

"I'll hold you. I promise not to let you fall."

She stepped toward him and placed her hands on his biceps, giving them a squeeze. "You definitely feel strong enough."

"Do you trust me?"

"Absolutely not. I've known you all of a half-hour, but I'd be a fool to pass up the chance to fly with an angel. Just don't drop me on anything sharp."

"Brave woman."

"Or incredibly stupid. I'll let you know which when we're done."

Snag your copy of Azrael at your favorite online retailer!

Watch for the other books in the
Speed Dating with the Denizens of the
Underworld Series

ASH

Lilith

The Morrígan

Orion

Hera

Abel

Odin

Mormos

Zeus

Michael

Váli

Apollo

Raphael

Baldur

Poseidon

Gabrielle

Frigg

Uriel

And More!

ASH

Macconwood Pack Novel Series

Macconwood Pack Tales

The Falk Clan Tales

The Bear Claw Tales

The Barvale Clan Tales

Purely Paranormal Pleasures

The Wardens of Terra

The Maverick Pride Tales

Dire Wolf Mates

Wyvern Protection Unit

EveL Worlds

The Guardians of Chaos

Howls Romance

Hearts of Stone

Accidentally Undead

Moongate Island Mates

Mated in Hope Falls

Island Stripe Pride

Standalones

C.D. GORRI

Barvale Holiday Tales

Shifter Unleashed Anthologies

Anthologies

ABOUT THE AUTHOR

C.D. Gorri is an USA Today Bestselling and Award-Winning author of steamy paranormal romance and urban fantasy. She is the creator of the Grazi Kelly Universe.

Join her mailing list here: https://www.cdgorri.com/newsletter.

ASH

An avid reader with a profound love for books and literature, when she is not writing or taking care of her family, she can usually be found with a book or tablet in hand. C.D. lives in her home state of New Jersey where many of her characters or stories are based. Her tales are fast paced yet detailed with satisfying conclusions.

If you enjoy powerful heroines and loyal heroes who face relatable problems in supernatural settings, journey into the Grazi Kelly Universe today. You will find sassy, curvy heroines and sexy, love-driven heroes who find their HEAs between the pages. Werewolves, Bears, Dragons, Tigers, Witches, Romani, Lynxes, Foxes, Thunderbirds, Vampires, and many more Shifters and supernatural creatures dwell within her worlds. The most important thing is every mate in this universe is fated, loyal, and true lovers always get their happily-ever-afters.

For a complete list of C.D. Gorri's books visit her website here: https://www.cdgorri.com/complete-book-list/

Thank you and happy reading!

del mare alla stella,
C.D. Gorri

ASH